# NZ Rugby Romance

Books 1 -5 Collection

EVA FOXX

**NZ Rugby Romance/ Eva Foxx**. -- 1st ed.
ISBN 978-0-6488502-2-9

To my very own Alpha – thank you

# CONTENTS

# JAXON

# Jaxon

Cool beads of sweat glide down my spine as my teammates and I make our way through the bustling streets of Auckland after practice.

The sun has descended below the horizon and grey clouds have begun to churn across the sky, the breeze carrying with it the smell of salt and brine from the nearby bay. The wind is cool tonight, signaling that it's going to rain yet again.

A few stars attempt to peek out between the dark clouds, but their radiance is swallowed almost completely. Despite the gloomy weather, the New Zealand city is alive tonight. People make their way between the busy shops and restaurants and bars, the sound of their laughter and chatter filling the streets. It reminds me of a beehive, the way the people zip back and forth.

"Go, Auckland!" shouts someone crossing the street, earning slurred cheers from intoxicated fans who've just stumbled out of a nearby bar.

We're rather recognizable in our telltale striped rugby uniforms. A few of my other teammates laugh and grin over at the fan.

Beside me, Ryder lifts a hand and waves. "Cheers, bro!" he shouts.

We'd only just finished practice a little bit ago, and now we're in pursuit of a hot plate of fish and chips and a nice cool beer. There's nothing better after hours spent racing across the rugby field.

"You reckon you'll come out with us this Friday, Jax?" Ryder asked, dragging a hand through his dark and still damp hair as he cocks his head to look at me. His eyes are blue as the water lapping at the Auckland coast.

"I don't spend more time with you lot than I have to," I snipe back, earning raucous laughter from Ryder and the rest of the team.

I'm the type of guy that enjoys my solitude.

I live for my rugby union team. I pour my heart and soul into the game just about every single day, but after that, I don't have much left over to give – not if I'm going to be selected for the Blues this season. It's the only way I'm going to be able to take that next step up to the All Blacks squad next year and become one of the youngest All Blacks players. That's been my goal since I was a kid, and it's one I intend to make good on.

Ryder rolls his eyes when I turn down yet another party. It's no surprise.

"You might be the best bloody player on the field," he quips, "but I'm the best bloody player off the field – if you get what I'm saying." Ryder cackles at his own joke and it's my turn to roll my eyes.

I lightly jab my elbow into his ribs and he chokes on his laughter. "I'd prefer my prize to be the national cup, not a girl in my bed."

"Then you've got your priorities confused, bro," he grins.

As the blokes around me again dissolve into laughter, my ears prick at the sound of distant shouting. Someone's in the middle of a heated argument.

I glance up, eyes tracking the noise until I spot a couple on the opposite corner of the street. They're standing close together, the man's arms lifting above his head. I can just barely make out the figure of a young blonde woman with her hands on her hips beside him.

"...Seriously thought you had what it took?" he's shouting, voice a snarling growl. "You're out of your mind!"

The woman seems to respond, but I can't hear what she says.

"That's a bit sus," Ryder murmurs, chin jerking toward the shouting couple. "Wonder what's going on. They're making heaps of noise."

When the man lurches toward the woman, my fingers curl into fists so tight my tan knuckles glow white. There's no way I can just stand back here on the sideline a moment longer. I've packed on muscle from rugby, might as well put it to good use.

I turn sharply and stalk straight across the street, ignoring the cars that slam on their brakes and blare their horns at me. The rest of the team pauses and stares after me, exchanging bewildered glances.

"How ya going?" I ask brusquely, wedging one brawny shoulder between the man and the woman. I don't yet look at the girl, glaring instead into the man's beady black eyes so he knows that I'm not about to let him sit here and go off on a woman.

"Good as gold. This ain't your bloody business," the man responds, trying to leer around my broad body at the woman behind me.

I shift so that I'm standing more securely in the way.

"You made it my bloody business when you picked a fight on my bloody street. Get out of here. I reckon you've made your point clear enough."

"You know what, you're right. I don't need this right now," he jerks sharply to the side to look around me one last time before thrusting an aggressive finger at the woman. "You're worthless, nothing but a waste of time. Always have been. Always will, Layla."

*Layla.*

The name strikes me like an arrow straight to the heart – or a sucker punch to the gut.

I blink hard, caught off guard by how much just that two syllable name sends shockwaves through my soul. It's a name that's lingered in the back of my mind for years, haunting nearly every dream I still have.

But there's no way the woman behind me could be that Layla – *my* Layla.

When I narrow my eyes on the man, he spits on the ground at my feet and whirls to stalk away.

Sighing, I grit my teeth and slowly turn toward the woman.

The sight of her makes my heart freeze in my chest.

A pair of wide green eyes that I thought I'd never see again gaze right back at me.

## CHAPTER TWO

# Layla

When I returned to New Zealand with my tail tucked between my legs, the last person I wanted to see was Jaxon.

I'd managed to convince myself that Auckland is big enough that I would be able to avoid him for a while, at least until I was back on my feet again.

Yet, as fate would have it, here he is on my very first night back.

He's as tall and broad and rugged as ever and my eyes can't help but wander over him.

The rugby uniform fits him like a glove... and those tiny shorts don't leave much to the imagination.

I swallow hard, biting my lower lip at the way the moon gleams on his perfectly chiseled legs. He's even sexier than he was when we first met just before uni, if that's possible. He must've recently finished up practice because his flesh is slightly shiny and his clothes are slightly damp. Every breath I take is flavored by his familiar cologne and grass and sweat.

The scent goes right to my head, making my mind spin like I'd had way too much rum.

When he clears his throat, I gulp and force myself to focus back on his face.

He looks as stunned as I am to have suddenly stumbled across one another again. His handsome face is familiar, yet different at the same time. His jaw is more square and sharp and his brown hair, longer now and curling against his forehead, is sun-streaked from long hours spent practicing rugby.

Has it really been years since I saw Jaxon?

Even after all this time, I can't help but think how easy it would be to step forward and melt into his arms. I want to rest my cheek on his chest and listen to his heart thrum against his ribs. I want to let my hands explore the dips and valleys of his muscled figure so that I can map out the differences of his body between now and then.

I first met Jax when I was eighteen. It was love at first sight, simple as that. The months that we spent together were short but glorious and filled with firsts.

I'd hoped he'd always remember me like that, a young girl with hope in her green eyes and a camera hanging around her neck, but I reckon that was shattered when he heard Charlie going off on me like that. Talk about embarrassing.

Then again, why the hell should I be embarrassed? I wasn't the one who'd insisted on throwing a fit in the middle of the street.

Riling up all over again at the thought to the way that scumbag was going off on me, I stomp around Jaxon.

"Fuck off, asshole!" I shout at Charlie. The man doesn't acknowledge me, still storming in the opposite direction.

When my mouth opens to continue on a further expletive diatribe, one of Jaxon's strong hands rests suddenly on my arm.

"He's probably heard enough, Layla."

When I frown up at Jaxon, a smirk has settled on his face. The shock has worn off now and has been replaced by curiosity, but I'm not prepared for his questions, of which there will surely be heaps.

When his fingers brush over my skin, electricity surges through me. It leaps from pore to pore, diving through my blood the way dolphins dive between shimmering waves.

I'm left panting, heart pounding and pulse racing. My nostrils flare as I try to catch my breath.

How can Jaxon still cause this kind of reaction in my body when I haven't looked into those beautiful golden eyes of his in so long?

It isn't fair.

I'd thought after I left that, eventually, I would forget how much I cared about him... how much I wanted him... but now those feelings have resurged with a vengeance. It's like they've fermented in my heart, growing stronger and stronger instead of dissipating.

"You want to tell me what that was about?" he prods.

I can't help but grimace. There it is; the questions. This is what I was afraid of.

A group of Jaxon's rugby buddies is loitering across the street. Though they'd been watching with keen interest while Jaxon confronted Charlie, now they'd begun calling Jaxon's name impatiently. He doesn't even seem to hear them. He's too focused on me. It's still the same, the way he makes me feel like I'm the center of the whole bloody world. I feel tears prickling the corners of my eyes and bite my lip, refusing to let them fall.

I can't cry. Not after what I did to him those years back.

I shake my head hard, hoping the movement will clear my watery eyes. "Yeah, no, Jaxon."

"I'm Jaxon now, not just Jax?" he muses. His eyes are becoming sad.

My lips part to argue that there was nothing '*just Jax*' about Jaxon. He's on his way to becoming a star rugby player... and who am I?

According to Charlie, I'm worthless.

I give up on the argument and purse my lips instead.

One of his russet eyebrows lifts and his smirk grows slightly more pronounced. "Was it a couples' spat? I suppose you have a habit of leaving spurned lovers in your wake, eh?"

The comment makes the hair on the back of my neck lift, but I don't argue that either. There isn't a point.

He appraises me briefly and then shrugs his massive shoulders – shoulders that I want to dig my fingernails into while he moans my name in my ear, clutching me against him with those iron-strong arms of his.

There's so much I could say to Jaxon, but my mouth refuses to move. My tongue feels glued against the roof of my mouth. I can only clutch my black photography bag against my side.

When his golden eyes pour into mine, a shiver rolls up my spine as heat begins to swell between my inner thighs. I press my knees hard together and try to keep my thoughts clean. A fat raindrop splashes suddenly on my cheek, and I'm grateful for the sky's cool blessing.

"The team is going to the club on Friday," he continues. "The preseason is almost over, so we want to celebrate before we find out who's selected to be on the Blues. You should come, Layla."

Oh god, I still love the way he says my name. He takes his take forming it with his perfect tongue, and when it leaves his lips, it makes me shudder again.

He looms over me, blocking out the fluorescent lights of nearby street signs. Everything else seems to fade away but the golden eyes gazing at me now.

"Um, I... I should go," I stammer hoarsely.

I don't want him to see my cheeks flushing red or the tears in my eyes or the confusion on my face. I take one step back before turning and dashing back down the road, my heels clicking beneath me.

No matter how much time has passed, it's still nearly impossible to turn my back on that man.

CHAPTER THREE

# Jaxon

My arms slowly fold over my chest as Layla turns a sharp corner and flees off into the night.

Layla's always running somewhere – usually away from me.

Watching her leave might be pleasurable, but I wish she was able to stay still for once in her life.

My heart gives an unexpected pang and I grimace in response. I lift my hand, brushing my fingers across the toned muscle of my pec. The ache deep in my chest stubbornly remains.

Even after all this time, she still manages to get under my skin.

I don't know why that surprises me. There's something special about Layla... and the way I feel about her. Since the first time I spotted her, I knew there was something about Layla that I wanted all to myself. It was far too easy to fall in love with her. That should have been the first red flag, but instead, I viewed it as a green light. I fell hard for her, tumbling head over heels the whole way. Gazing into those eyes of hers, I could open up in ways I never had before.

She was the first person I ever told about wanting to become an All Blacks player for the Auckland Rugby Union team. I'd expected her to laugh. I mean, how many young boys said exactly what I had? But she hadn't laughed. Instead, she'd twined her fingers with mine and squeezed my hand and whispered, "I know you can do it."

Every detail of that precious night is still etched into my head. It plays in my dreams like a movie reel.

With only a few mere weeks before uni began, Layla and I had decided to go camping near a secluded beach. It was just us and the stars and the quiet crash of waves on golden sand. The night had been cool, but we'd found ways to make it hotter.

I should have known then that our time together was too amazing to last.

She vanished not too long after that steamy night.

One day, she was at my side, and the next, she was gone.

I showed up at her house to pick her up for another night of camping, but she wasn't there. I had to find out from her mother that she'd gone all the way to Sydney to pursue photography. She'd never even mentioned it to me, aside from snapping pictures of me every chance she got.

Ryder's voice suddenly pierces through the haze of my memory.

"Bro! That was brutal! Now I see why you never come out with us – you can't get a girl even if you save her life, eh?" Ryder throws his head back, slapping a hand against his abs as he laughs.

The rain is beginning to fall harder now. The cool drops soak through my striped jersey and make a chill shiver through me. A low rumble of thunder echoes through the city streets. The people that were buzzing about flock into open doors to escape the torrent.

Slowly, I turn away from where I'd been gazing down the street after Layla and head back toward the guys waiting for me.

Ryder is smiling from ear to ear. He doesn't seem to mind the rain. In fact, he seems to rather enjoy being soaked to the bone. "Come on, Jax! Let's get you a beer to soothe your trouble."

I just roll my eyes and join in the guys' laughter. It's easier to chuckle along with them than try to explain that my teenage sweetheart had just reappeared in the city she left behind years ago. That would be way too long of a story to share with the rugby boys.

Even though I try to put the evening behind me, every time I blink, I still see the image of Layla's face on the backs of my eyelids like it's been seared there. I can't help but dissect her expression, trying to find the reason she'd returned to New Zealand in her emerald eyes. It was her eyes that haunted me the most. In them was a faint sadness where once cheerful delight shone, but that didn't change the fact that she'd become more gorgeous than ever. She'd always been beautiful, but now she was even more so.

At just the sight of her, my heart had begun to batter against my ribs. I'd been so sure I was dreaming that I almost wanted to pinch myself. That guy who was shouting at her is lucky that I didn't realize it was Layla he was yelling at, or else he would've gotten a serious hiding. I have a feeling he wouldn't dare show up again after I told him off though.

Why was he shouting at her like that, anyway?

I can't help but reckon that there's some part of Layla's puzzle that I'm missing, but then again, she's always been a bit of a mystery. She can't be bothered to wear her heart on her sleeve. I'd learned that lesson the hard way.

Ryder nudges me in the ribs. "By the way, did I hear you say something about us going out this Friday, bro? You finally ready to hang out with us lot?"

"Yeah... I think so," I answer, hiding my grin.

"Awesome," answered Ryder. "It's about time you had some fun."

I nod, glancing back toward the direction Layla had headed in.

I have no idea if she'll show up on Friday... but suddenly I'm a whole lot more interested in how that night might go.

## CHAPTER FOUR

# Layla

Music pulses from inside the club.

The beat throbs to the rhythm of my heart, making my pulse race even faster than it already is.

What the hell am I even doing here?

When I'd dashed away from Jaxon a few nights ago, I'd promised myself that I would avoid him at all costs until I could leave Auckland again... but now here I am, outside the very club that he said he'd be at this very moment.

So much for that.

The whole way over here, I tried to tell myself that I was only interested in seeing Jaxon again because this may be our only chance. I had my ticket booked and I'd be on the next flight out of here. By the time the sun came up, I'd be watching the sunrise from a jet window. It's not like I can stay.

Jaxon has his whole career ahead of him and I... well, I have other things that I need to focus on.

"G'day, babe," a deep voice suddenly purrs from behind me.

Before I can react, a strong arm slips around my waist. I twist away from the foreign hold, glowering up into the blue eyes of the guy trying to make a move on me.

"How ya going?" he asks, undeterred by the growing glower on my face.

I recognize his cheerfully oblivious face as one of the rugby guys watching Jaxon and I interact the other night. He doesn't appear to recognize me, however. I can tell immediately that he's the type of guy who believes he's God's gift to women – and, unfortunately, he's handsome enough that most girls probably do fall at his feet. He's got an ego even bigger than Auckland, I would reckon.

"Aren't you hotter than the New Zealand sun," he continues with a pearly smile even I have to admit is charming despite his horrible pickup line. "The name's Ryder. Wouldn't you like to ride something sexy tonight?"

I narrow my eyes on his. "Not even. And if you so much as touch me again, I'll kick you right in the-"

"Okay, now" another voice interjects, but this time I recognize the speaker.

My heart is in my throat as I twist my head up to gaze into Jaxon's familiar golden eyes, though he isn't meeting my startled stare. Instead, he's taking in the short, tight black dress and black heels I'd opted to wear tonight. The heat of his eyes blaze up my long legs, and I find  myself wanting to bask in his gaze forever.

Maybe I'd dolled up a little, but definitely not just for him. That would just be silly.

"Ain't you a feisty one!" laughs Ryder. He looks over at Jax and smirks. "I'd be careful if I were you, bro. I reckon you'll be in way over your head with her!"

"You might be right," Jaxon murmurs, more to himself than to Ryder. "But you go on ahead, we'll be right behind you."

*We.*

Something about the way he says it so casually makes my pores want to start steaming again.

Ryder nods, winking at me one last time before prancing in through the club doors. When the doors open for the rugby player, the music echoes louder for a moment. When the doors shut again, it becomes quiet on the street.

Jaxon and I are alone again, aside from the people wandering up and down the sidewalk. I glance around, watching some of the girls cast hungry looks at Jax. A possessiveness that I have no right to feel prickles up the back of my neck. I don't want anyone looking at Jax like that.

"You came," Jax notes simply. His expression is one of careful nonchalance.

I shrug and nervously tuck a lock of hair behind my ear. "Eh, I was just passing by."

He gives a pointed look at my outfit and a blush sears over my cheeks. My white lie wasn't convincing in the slightest. I don't even know why I tried.

Then, slowly, Jaxon closes the already short distance between us.

He leans against the wall beside me, his broad body dwarfing mine.

My mind begins to whirl again. The nostalgic fragrance of his cologne washes over me like a tidal wave, threatening to drag me back into his arms. I can remember wearing his shirt wrapped around my naked body and burying my face against the soft fabric, breathing in that comforting, exhilarating smell.

My throat goes dry and I stare down at my feet.

It was a mistake to come here.

Can I really only have just one more night with Jaxon? It would never be enough. I'm accomplishing nothing but torturing myself.

"Anyway, I have an early morning so I should be going," I stammer, taking one step away, but Jaxon reaches out and lightly grabs my arm.

The hold is tight and warm but not threatening, and his touch is enough to make fireworks burst across my vision. My whole stomach clenches, heat coiling deep in my core. The pulsing of the music inside the club no longer beats just to the racing of my heart, but also to the throbbing lust deep inside my body.

Unable to even bear the thought of pulling away from him and having his hot touch leave my body, my feet inch back closer to him instead. He leans down, breath hot on my ear as he whispers, "You came all this way. Have just one dance with me... for old time's sake."

My chin dips into a nod before I can even register what's going on.

It's not as if I had a choice. I've never been able to say no to Jaxon... that's part of the reason why I left without ever saying goodbye.

CHAPTER FIVE

# Jaxon

Layla's hand fits perfectly in mine as I pull her toward the dance floor. Though she'd seemed hesitant to come into the club at first, now there's no resistance at all in the way she moves with me.

In the dim lights of the club, it's so easy to imagine that we're teenagers again and that life is as simple and straightforward as it was when she and I first met.

A faint rainbow of lights flashes over the floor as I pull her closer. She gazes at me, green eyes locked on mine, and her body slowly presses against me. My hands slip down her sides, heading toward her hips. I can feel the alluring warmth of her flesh through the thin fabric of her black dress.

She gives a quiet sigh that's swallowed up by the music, though I find myself leaning closer to hear the sweet sound that I've only dreamt about for the last few years.

I've missed Layla so much the last few years, but it was the oddest things that I missed most. Her laugh, the way she'd sigh while deep in thought, the click of her favorite heels on the sidewalk, or the way she'd squeal when she found a beautiful shell on the beach... those were the things I longed to hear most.

Back then, we'd dance just like this beneath the stars. There was no music, but we'd sway to the beat of our hearts.

Her palms splay out flat against my pecs, though when the first song ends and the next begins, her rebel fingers begin exploring my body. I reckon my rugby mates ae around somewhere, but I don't care whether they see me or not. Besides, they'd just be jealous that I have someone as beautiful as Layla in my arms. Ryder's mind is probably blown right now, if he hasn't found some other girl in the club to lavish with heaps of attention – for one night, at least.

I close my eyes as the music swells. Our swaying becomes slower and slower even as the song picks up pace. Her hips grind against mine as her head finds my shoulder. Her breath is warm and shallow against my neck. I grip her against me, one hand on the small of her back while the other cups the perfect curve of her ass. She gives another quiet moan, clinging to my shirt. Her dress is so dangerously short that, if I wanted to, it'd be a simple move to slip my hand beneath her dress.

Her hips grind against me again and I can feel the heat between her thighs.

The hand at her back glides up to cup her face. I lift her head, the tip of my nose brushing hers.

She had to know wearing this tiny black dress would torture me. You can make out every curve of her body and, judging by the hardened nipples straining against the fabric, I doubt she's wearing a bra. She may not even be wearing panties either.

The stray thought makes all my blood pool south. I grit my jaw, clenching her against me. She bites her lip when my throbbing manhood presses against her. She grinds against me again, her eyes hooded and pupils dilated. Our faces are only inches apart.

I could kiss her... but I don't want our first kiss after so long to be in this club.

"Ready to get out of here, eh?" I ask huskily. "My flat is close."

She nods, wetting her lips, and her hand again slides into mine as I lead her back out onto the sidewalk. Her fingers tightly lace with mine.

Only minutes later, we're stumbling into my flat.

Though I'd once shared the space with Ryder and some of the other guys, I'd recently opted to get my own space. I'm glad for it now because Layla and I can have the place all to ourselves.

We don't even make it all the way over the threshold before I pull her up and into my arms, her legs twining around my waist. I twist, slamming the door shut and locking it before pressing her against the wall. She moans, hips still grinding against mine as I pin her arms up over her head against the wall.

I press my forehead to hers, gazing deep into her beautiful green eyes that churn with lust. Then, I press her against the wall more firmly and my mouth dips to press to hers.

Kissing Layla causes an explosion of pleasure and desire to detonate inside my core. I moan against her lips, my tongue begging for entrance. The velvet tip of her own pink tongue greets mine, and I deepen the kiss.

We kiss until our lungs are screaming for air, but when we part, it's only for the briefest of seconds before we return again to each other's lips. The moment is so perfect that I would again think I was dreaming if it wasn't for the sweltering heat building between us now.

I'm rock-hard and dying to fuck Layla, but I want tonight to last as long as it can.

Her chest heaves as I glide her dress up and over her hips. As I'd thought, there's nothing beneath it but her tan, captivating flesh.

I lift her up off the wall, my fingers digging into her ass as I carry her to the bedroom and gently throw her down on the bed. She writhes with lust, dress hiked around her waist. I tear off my clothes before descending upon her. I kiss my way up her tan leg, taking all the time in the world to savor the flavor of her skin against my tongue and lips.

By the time I pause between her inner thighs, her fingers are knotted in my hair and her hips are desperately grinding toward my face. I grin, pushing her thighs roughly apart so that I can taste her innermost flavor.

My tongue drags up her drenched slit and she cries out, grinding against my face. I pin her against the bed, eyes all but rolling back when she begins to loudly moan my name. After all this time, I still know how to make her scream with ecstasy.

When all of her muscles contract at once and her cries rise to a fever pitch, I drink in all she has to offer before climbing further up her body.

Layla is breathless, her hair in her eyes as she smiles up at me wolfishly.

She leans up, mouth capturing mine as I tear her dress off her body. I want to see all of her. I want to touch as much as I can of her.

My hips sink between her legs, the tip of my engorged manhood begging for her.

Slowly, I thrust inside of her. Her velvet inner walls greet me, tight and slick around my cock. I thrust, fireworks bursting in front of my eyes.

"Jax..." she cries, holding onto me as tight as she can. "You feel so bloody good...!"

I love hearing her call my name. Primal greed overtakes me as I roughly thrust into her. Each powerful stroke is longer and harder than the last. In this moment, Layla belongs completely to me. She is mine and mine alone, as she should be.

Again and again, her inner muscles contract around me, her body shaking with pleasure.

I pin her down, ravishing her lips until I can take no more.

Then I bury myself within her one final time and we collapse in a damp, blissful heap.

## CHAPTER SIX

# Layla

Stars still twinkle outside Jax's window when my eyes slowly drift open.

I'd been awake for some time already, but I'd been pretending that I could lay here forever and not have to worry about what hour it is. I hold my breath, staring forward as the moon peers curiously back. There isn't a cloud in the sky tonight and the deep navy hues of evening are just beginning to melt away. Soon, streaks of orange and magenta will glow across the horizon.

By then, I'll be on a plane.

My eyes squeeze shut again as the pair of strong arms around my naked waist tighten slightly, drawing me back against the muscled chest pressed to my spine. We'd slept perfectly curled together, waking occasionally to share kisses or to roll across the sheets.

Last night was, I reckon, the best night of sleep I'd gotten since I left New Zealand to head to Sydney.

Usually, I toss and turn, like my brain can't be bothered to relax for more than a few seconds at a time, but I'd slept like a baby while I was wrapped nice and tight in Jax's strong arms. His years of playing rugby have left him muscled and strong and I'd had little choice but to feel snug in his embrace.

How would I ever work up the strength to leave now? It'd been hard enough the first time.

I can remember that plane ride too. It was an early morning just like this, and I'd gazed out the window down at Auckland and wept the entire way. The other passengers had cast sympathetic glances in my direction, but I knew I didn't deserve their sympathy.

Jax sighs in his sleep and nuzzles his face against the nape of my neck. My heart shatters in my chest at his sweet affection.

It's only with him that I feel this safe and secure and wanted. No one else has ever compared to Jax's memory. I've hardly even wanted another man to touch me, Jax left such a tender imprint on my heart and soul. Being beside him now makes me feel dangerously whole again.

This is the moment I've been waiting for and dreaming about since I walked away from him... but I can't stay.

I have to leave.

He needs to get back to his life now, he needs to get back to his team and his own ambitions. He doesn't need a reminder of the past lingering any longer.

As carefully as possible, I unwind myself from his arms. I pause every few seconds and listen closely to make sure that his breathing remains even and deep. I don't want to have to explain why I need to leave yet again.

Once freed, I scurry silently across the room, picking up what I can find of my clothes. In the end, I abandon one of my heels. I'll pick up a pair of jandals on my way to the airport.

When my fingers brush the doorknob of the flat and begin to twist it open, a strong hand suddenly thrusts the wooden door shut again. The doorframe shakes with the force of the movement.

I jump, whirling around and coming face to face with Jaxon.

He takes a step back, arms folding over his broad, still naked chest as he frowns at me. His golden eyes are furious, though I understand his anger. Waning moonlight floods in through the windows and casts the room with a silver glow.

"Is this just what you do, Layla?" Jax asks. His voice is deep and gruff. "You just run off when you've had your fill?"

"No, Jax. I-"

"What?" he interjects. "How else could you explain what's happening right now?"

He throws his arms in the air and turns his back to me, shaking his head as he stares out across the disordered room where he and I had kissed in every corner last night. When he turns back, his eyes are no longer furious. Instead, they're filled with a hollow sadness that shakes me to the core.

Is this the way he looked when I left the first time?

I've hurt him again.

Is that all that I'm good for?

"I..." I whisper helplessly. I don't have an answer that will make him happy. I don't have an explanation for how I treated him that will help heal his pain.

He moves closer, though he keeps a sliver of distance between us.

"Did you just not care about me back then, Layla? Is that why you never said goodbye? Do you still not care?"

"Of course I do!" I cry out. "Jax, you don't understand. I care about you so much that I-"

"So much that you're going to sneak away just like you did before?" he interrupts in a flat, stern tone.

I swallow hard, floundering for some other explanation, but Jax is just becoming angrier.

His golden eyes narrow. "You've already left me without a goodbye once. I have no idea why I expected things to be different this time around. I didn't know what to expect after last night, but I thought I'd at least be worthy of a real goodbye."

Tears are beginning to sting at the corners of my eyes. I fight them, but one falls and glides down my cheek, leaving a hot trail behind it. "You're worthy of so much, Jax."

"Wait, is this what happened with that other guy too? You led him on and then tried to vanish and it backfired on you?"

"No," I whisper, stepping forward. "That isn't what happened with Charlie. I never touched him. Not once."

Instinctively, I reach out to comfort Jax. My hands press against his chest, but his frown only becomes more stark. He pulls away as though my touch burned his tan skin, dragging his hands through his hair.

I can't handle being the one to have hurt him like this. The first time I left, I hadn't said goodbye because no explanation would be good enough and I knew I couldn't leave him if I tried to say goodbye face to face.

But now, I can't run from the truth. Not anymore.

Now, I have no choice but to tell him.

"I'm a failure, Jax," I whisper hoarsely, more tears welling in my eyes. "That's why I had to leave. That's why I disappeared. You are destined for so many wonderful things... but you heard Charlie, I'm worthless!"

# Jaxon

Layla's face is pinched and pained and her voice breaks as she forces word after painful word to leave her sweet lips.

When she's finished, she slumps back against the wall as if it'd taken all of her power just to speak. I grab her, keeping her standing while her sad eyes shift slowly up toward mine. Her lower lip trembles and she bites it hard to make it stop.

"What do you mean you're a failure, Layla?"

All of my anger vanished the moment Layla said that single word. How anyone as talented or special as Layla could view themselves as worthless blows my mind. The world hadn't been kind to her since she left New Zealand.

"You can't be the one trying to make me feel better, Jax," she whispers while trying to push away my hands. "I'm the one that disappeared. Remember?"

"Believe me, I reckon I'll never be able to forget the way I felt when I found out you were gone, Layla... but that doesn't matter right now. What matters is the truth. Tell me what happened. Tell me why you left. Put it all out in the open, eh?"

The green-eyed woman drags in a ragged breath but finally nods.

"...When you and I first got together, I was waiting to hear back from a prestigious photography program nearby. I was positive I'd get in, Jax. I'd never been more sure about anything. You were climbing up the ranks of the junior rugby team and I was so proud of you... Everyone was talking about how you'd be the next All Blacks star soon enough." She pauses and winces, "But then I found out I didn't get into that program. I wasn't even waitlisted. I was flat out rejected. I couldn't face you. Not when you were so gifted and brilliant and I... I was-"

"Don't you dare say worthless again, Layla," I hiss quietly.

She drags a hand across her teary eyes and sniffles. "I was so ashamed that I'd failed. I didn't think I deserved to be next to you when you had so much promise and I didn't. So, I went to Sydney. There was another program there that I wanted to try to get into, but I ended up getting discouraged and giving up before I even finished applying. Soon after that, I met Charlie."

"The bloke that was shouting at you?"

She nods. "He was a photographer with a popular studio in Sydney. I was shocked that he noticed me. He took me under his wing and began to mentor me. For a while, it was amazing. I was learning a lot and Charlie was always telling me all about the prizes I would win and the exhibits I would be part of... but as time went on, I realized that things weren't adding up. There were no prizes. There were no exhibits. I was about to walk away from him when he told me that he was opening a new studio here in New Zealand and he wanted me to be the star of it all. I thought maybe, just maybe, it was finally my time to shine."

Layla gives a feeble laugh and shakes her head. I cup her cheek and she sighs before continuing to speak.

"We flew into Auckland Airport and that's when it became clear that if I wanted to be part of his studio, I would have to... prove myself in ways completely unrelated to photography."

The hair on the back of my neck lifts as fury begins to simmer in my core. I could read between the lines. I knew exactly what that Charlie guy wanted from Layla. If I ever saw him again, he'd get a straight hiding.

My thumb brushes her cheek and she places her hand overtop mine. "I told Charlie no, and the result of that conversation is what you witnessed in the street. After leaving you that night, I immediately booked a ticket out of town."

"You're going back to Australia?" I ask, voice strained.

She hesitates and shakes her head. "No... I'm going to London."

I grip her shoulders and lean down so that I can gaze back into her eyes. "Why do you have to go so far, Layla? Why are you always running? Why do you have to put so much distance between us?"

"Because I want to be with you, Jax!" she cries hoarsely. "Because when I'm trying to forget just how badly I want to be with you!"

My fingers tighten on her slender shoulders. "If you want to be with me, then be with me! I don't think you're worthless. Don't you see that? I know you're talented. I know you're worthy. I care more about you than anything else. Rugby can be bloody damned for all I care. I'd rather have you than anything else!"

Layla's breath hitches, her eyes widening. "Even after I left, you still feel that way?"

"I reckon I'll feel that way until the day I die, Layla," I respond firmly. "I love you. I always have. Always will. You're a part of my bloody soul. You're ingrained in my heart. Everything I am, everything I do, it's in part because I got to know you. It's because you're a piece of me."

"Jax..." she whispers, more tears pouring down her cheeks. She flings out her arms, wrapping me up in an embrace so tight that I can feel her heart pounding against her ribs.

I hold her, stroking her hair as she weeps into my shoulder.

"I love you too," she cries. "I thought... I just assumed that after everything, you'd never want me. I thought I lost you forever when I walked away. Ever since I left, I've regretted my decision. I wished I'd stayed. Auckland is where I was born... but your arms are my home."

"Then stay forever in them," I whisper into her hair. "We can chase our dreams together. When one of us slips, the other will be there to catch them. We can support one another, Layla, instead of running."

She lifts her head, cupping my face. She nods breathlessly, pressing her forehead to mine.

"Yes, Jax... I won't let anything come between us again. I won't run anymore."

"Good, because next time I won't let you slip away so easily. Now that I have you in my arms, I never want to let you go."

I lean closer, pressing my lips to hers, and she runs her fingers through my hair while kissing me back. We sink down against the floor, wrapped tight in one another's embrace.

Though no one can say for sure what tomorrow will bring, the one thing I'm sure about is that each day Layla and I spend together will be far happier than                    the                    last.

# Layla

"You took this shot, bro?" gasps Ryder. He gestures at the photo of the beach hanging on the wall. Shells glimmer across the sand like stars in the sky. "Straight up?"

"Straight up," I grin back at the blue-eyed rugby player, pretending not to notice that he'd referred to me as 'bro.' Then again, I suppose it's a compliment coming from Ryder.

He just gasps again and turns back to the framed photo.

I pause to look around, eyes misting as I take in the various photographs I'd snapped that hang on the walls of the cozy gallery. It's a small space, but I'm proud of it... and it's only just the beginning for me. I'd already heard from a few magazines that want to publish my photos. I was finally finding my way in the world of photography.

Suddenly, across the room, I'm snared by a pair of golden eyes that never cease to leave me breathless.

Jax crosses the gallery in a few short and powerful strides before sweeping me up into his powerful arms. He dips me backward, kissing me warmly. When he rights me again, my head is spinning from the sweetness of his kiss. I cling to his jacket, smiling dazedly up at the love of my life.

Has it already been a year since Jax and I reconnected? It's flown by like seconds.

"Sorry I'm late, love," he murmurs into my ear. "I just got a phone call from the coach."

"The coach?" I whisper, trying to keep myself from jumping up and down out of excitement. "What did he say?"

Jax pulls me into his arms and rests his forehead against mine. "I didn't want to mention it tonight. This is your night, Layla... but I did it... I made it onto the All Blacks!"

I can't help the thrilled squeal that tears from my lungs. I throw my arms up around his neck and he laughs, spinning me around. A few of the people in the gallery look over and smile as they watch us.

My heart is so full that I can hardly believe it.

"This is the best day of my life!" I laugh, gazing into Jax's eyes. Suddenly, his happy face gets a little somber. "...What's wrong, Jax?"

He doesn't answer, simply slowly sinking down so that he's kneeling on the ground. A few people gasp and my own hands fly to my face as he pulls a small velvet box from his pocket. He flips it effortlessly open and a diamond ring twinkles in the studio lights.

"Layla... this last year has been the happiest of my life. You've made me want to be a better man and a better rugby player. For over three hundred and sixty-five days, we've been inseparable. If you would be beside me for every single day from here on out for the rest of our lives, I would be the luckiest man-"

"Yes!" I cry before he can even finish his tender speech. I fling myself down at him, nearly tackling him to the ground.

He laughs and cradles me in his strong arms.

"Yes! Yes! Yes, yes, yes, Jax! You're my soulmate and my other half. You support me at every turn and remind me every day how lucky I am to have you in my life. I would love to marry you!"

He slides the ring on my finger and then presses his lips to mine as people take pictures on their phones. Though I'd built a career as a photographer, it would be those photos I treasured most for the rest of my life.

Returning to Auckland was one of the hardest things I'd ever done, but it'd led me straight into the arms of the man I'd never stopped loving. The only thing that makes me even more deliriously happy than being in my fiancé's arms is the thought of what the future will bring us as husband and wife.

The End

# KAI

## CHAPTER ONE

# Kai

Ice cold water seeps across my face, the thin rivulets streaking across my tanned cheeks and over the tattoos on my muscled chest. I lift the water bottle a little higher, opening my mouth to gulp in a swig of the frigid liquid.

Overhead, the sun is big and bright and impossibly hot. Even the green grass of the rugby practice field has wilted. Now it crackles beneath our shoes every time we charge powerfully back and forth while we're running intense drills over and over. A few men still amble around, passing the ball back and forth to get in some extra practice despite the heat. I reckon we've already been out here for hours. I'm bloody lucky for my Maori blood, or else I'd be red as a lobster.

Rugby practice is practically lethal in this New Zealand weather – but we live for it.

When I first decided to pursue a professional career in rugby, everyone thought I was crazy – especially my father. He all but disowned me from the family when I joined the union team. Every day, I end up wondering if I made the right choice.

"Kai!"

I whip toward the familiar sound of one of my teammates calling my name. Beads of cool water drip from my long, dark lashes.

Ryder grins at me, one arm hooked around Jax's neck. The two blokes are in the middle of roughhousing, as was usual of anyone who wandered too close to playful, energetic Ryder. Even though the heat is suffocating, my best friend is as spirited as ever. Jax looks a little less enthused.

"Jax is trying to spin quite the yarn over here!" Ryder shouts.

A few other players look on now, watching curiously as Jax rolls his eyes and tries to wrench away from Ryder's hold. Ryder stubbornly holds on.

"Straight up?" I answer, shaking my head so that the cool water I'd dumped all over my head sprayed in every direction. The droplets cast a rainbow of light as they fly from my dark hair.

Ryder laughs loudly and nods. "He's pretending that nothing happened with the hot girl he danced with at the club the other night, but that's awful sus coming from Jax, eh? He never dances with anyone. Hell, he barely even ever goes out with us!"

Finally able to break away, Jax smirks at Ryder. "Sounds to me like you're just jealous."

"Not even," pouts Ryder. "And does that mean you're admitting something's going on, bro?"

Jax's face turns a little more red as he shrugs his burly shoulders. As mischievous as Ryder can be, I reckon he might just be on to something when it comes to Jax and his mystery woman. Still, it was nice to see Jax joking around. The guy was usually so serious, focused only on making the All Blacks squad as soon as he could. I understood his drive to be the best of the best. He's certainly not the only one on this team to feel that way.

Ryder darts away when Jax playfully pushes at him and trots across the field toward me.

"Well, if Jax has found a lady friend, at least I can count on you to still be my wingman, eh?" he says with a grin.

Ryder and I have known one another since we were kids playing rugby for the junior league. While I tend to be reserved and quiet, he's loud and a little crass. Maybe it's our differences that have made such good friends. We certainly have different desires in life. While Ryder spends all his spare time chasing girls, I'm only keen on one girl in particular... even though I'll never be able to have her.

She's unattainable and forbidden despite my yearning for her.

I've never voiced aloud how much I want her. I can't. It'd ruin everything.

Ryder pauses, his blue eyes abruptly focusing on something behind me.

"Look who came to visit us lot!" Ryder calls happily.

He charges across the field, wrapping a plump and petite young woman into a tight hug.

"You're all sweaty, Ryder!" shrieks the cute girl as she squirms out of Ryder's embrace. "Let go!"

"G'day, Jade!" Jax calls. He's picked up a rugby ball and is practicing tossing it up into the air and catching it.

She waves at Jax once Ryder releases her and then shields the sun off her face with one of her hands to gaze up at Ryder.

"When my little sister comes out to watch me play, I know it's going to be a good day!" the playful rugby player announces jovially.

Jade says something in response, but I'm too busy watching the way the sunlight reflects off her long, dark locks to listen. Her hair gleams like an ebony raven wing in the afternoon light.

It might just be the most beautiful thing I've ever seen.

My throat goes tight as I take in the way her blue cotton sundress clings to her curves in all the right places.

Jade is my unattainable, forbidden desire. She has been since I can remember.

To Ryder, she might just be his little sister, but to me, she's all woman. Every time Jade comes by the rugby field, I have a hard time catching my breath. Even though Ryder and I have known one another since our youth, I've never looked at Jade like a sister. To me, she's always been her own beautiful person, a person I want so badly to get close to.

If Ryder knew the way I felt, he'd give me a hiding. He'd never forgive me. Jade is his world, and he has no problem loudly proclaiming that.

For that reason, I've kept myself carefully guarded when it comes to Jade. I don't talk to her and I don't engage with her. Hell, I barely even bloody look at her. Even a glance is dangerous. When I lock eyes with her, it takes all my might just to look away again.

I know I shouldn't want my best friend's little sister, but I've never craved anything like I crave the chance just to be with her.

## CHAPTER TWO

# Jade

Heat pools in my core, and it isn't just because of the blinding sun in the sapphire sky.

The sun's rays dazzle my eyes, leaving black spots flickering in my vision, but when I blink, they erupt with a fiery crimson glow.

Even though I haven't glanced across the field yet, I can feel *him* looking in my direction.

I wish I could say the only reason I come out to visit my brother during his practices is because Ryder and I are the only family that we have left and we should support one another... but in all honesty, it's because I want to see more of the dark-haired, dark-eyed Maori rugby player that Ryder considers a brother.

Kai is the very definition of tall, dark, and handsome.

While I'm petite and curvy, he looms over much of the rugby team. His shoulders are broad and strong and tanned and his jaw is so sharp it could cut diamonds. Ever since I can remember, just the sight of him makes butterflies whirl around my stomach. Even when I was too young to know what true attraction felt like, he still made my whole body tingle. And his laugh... I can't get enough of his laugh. Sometimes when Kai is visiting Ryder, I can hear him chuckling from across the flat and it makes my head spin.

He never laughs when I'm around. Hell, Kai hardly talks.

Ryder insists Kai is just shy, but I think it's because my brother's best friend hates me. I don't know what I did to offend Kai, but it can't be a coincidence that when I enter a room, he leaves. Even now, Kai has turned toward his gear that's across the field so he can go.

Kai and my older brother have been best friends for years and Kai probably looks at me like a kid just like my big brother does, but I wish Kai knew how I really felt. My childhood crush has bloomed into a deep, raw longing that will never be satisfied.

After all, how would I ever tell Ryder how I felt about Kai? After our parents died, Ryder and I only had one another, and Ryder considers Kai a brother. How could I come between that?

Then again, it's not like Kai wants me like I want him. He can't stand me.

I steal one, longing look at Kai. The man is walking away, his broad body swaying back and forth. He's shirtless and his damp skin glows under the sun. Those tiny, sexy rugby shorts fit him perfectly. His tan chest has tattoos that slither over his muscled pecs, and sometimes I fantasize about how it would feel to map them out with my own fingers.

Why won't he even look at me?

Maybe if his mysterious eyes locked on mine just once, I could let go of this intense craving I have for him.

A rebellious chill rolls up my spine despite the heat.

"Are you ready?" I ask Ryder, forcing myself to tear my eyes away from Kai.

"Ready?" Ryder echoes blankly before his eyes widen and his whole face falls. "Yeah, no, Jade," he groans. "I totally forgot that I promised Jax I would run extra drills with him today. You know how he is about that. I can try to tell him I can't be bothered today and-"

"It's all good," I mutter, forcing a smile as I interrupt Ryder's speech.

The fact that my older brother forgot this annual ritual stings, but it doesn't surprise me. Lately, it feels like he's completely moved on and I'm the only one left in the past spinning my wheels.

"I was just hoping you and I could talk about my plans for uni," I continue. "The deadline is coming up for the nursing program I want to get into and-"

This time it's Ryder who interrupts me.

"Nursing program?" He eyes me, one eyebrow quirking upward. "What's left to talk about, eh? It ain't a good idea. It's too risky."

I blink hard to avoid rolling my eyes. "It's not risky, Ryder. It's about helping people. The medical team tried so hard to save Mum and Dad after their accident and I want to be like them!"

Ryder's jaw clenches. "It is risky! You could catch some crazy illness or something, Jade. Pick a safer program... like, I don't bloody care, teaching."

We stare at one another, neither blinking or backing down an inch. I don't understand Ryder's reluctance to hold me back from my dream any more than he seems to understand my desire for it.

Then Ryder sighs and shoots a stare across the field. "Hey! Kai! Get your ass over here."

Kai, looking perplexed, slowly turns and jogs back toward us. I can't stop staring at the way his powerful muscles strain and tense with every move he makes. He all but glides across the grass. By the time he's made it over, my knees are shaking and my head is spinning. He's so gloriously good-looking it's ridiculous.

"How ya going, bro?" Kai asks, dragging a hand through his dark hair.

Naturally, Kai doesn't look at me. It's like I'm invisible. I cross my arms self-consciously over my plump figure and dig my shoe into the ground. Maybe I'm just not his type. Then again, would that be surprising? He's sexy and successful and I'm just his best friend's curvy little sister.

Ryder claps Kai on the shoulder. "Listen, Jade and I had plans tonight but I have to bail. Can you go with her? I know you'll take good care of her."

My jaw drops, heart throbbing out of shock.

A chance to be alone with Kai? It's almost too good to be true, but there's no way Kai would ever agree to it. Deepening my shock, Kai shrugs his massive shoulders.

"I reckon I can do that," says Kai. He pauses and, for just a moment, his eyes finally pouring into mine. "I'll take real good care of her."

I'd thought gazing into Kai's dark eyes would free me from my captivation of him, but I was so very wrong.

I'm falling more than ever for my brother's best friend.

## CHAPTER THREE

# Kai

Jade and I silently walk away from the practice rugby field toward the parking lot where much of the team's cars still sit.

The beautiful, curvy young woman has been oddly quiet since Ryder pawned her off on me, though that's probably because she's irked over Ryder abandoning their plans. I reckon no one's ever accused Ryder of being too dependable.

I clear my throat, trying to come up with something to say, but I'd devoted so much time and effort to avoiding Jade that being alone with her now feels strained and awkward... if only because I'm still fighting the urge to touch her. It would be so easy to reach out and lace my fingers with hers or hook my arm around her waist and pull her against me.

On the pavement, our shadows lope forward, their figures bouncing together with every step we take. I never thought I'd be envious of my own shadow.

Even if I could touch her, I'm not sure she'd want me to. I'm rough around the edges and gruff, and she would probably want someone more tender and gentle. I don't even know what it means to be gentle. There's no room for that on the rugby field.

"Um..." Jade says abruptly, "I don't have my car here. I had a friend drop me off. Ryder was supposed to drive."

I jerk my chin toward my own car parked not too far away. When we get closer, I yank open the passenger door for her. She looks up at me with faint surprise in her eyes before sliding into the seat. A second later, we're steering down the road.

When I turn toward the city, she points in the other direction toward a winding pass of dirt roads that go through green fields and tall trees.

"Actually, we should head away from the city," she says. "It's not far and I know the way."

This is interesting to me. I'd assumed that when Ryder said to take her out, that I'd be treating her to some fancy dinner or something. Considering my sweaty, rugby-clothed state, this is definitely a better choice.

Following her directions, I drive us up and down hills and around fields. By the time she's signaled us to pull to a stop, the sun has begun to melt toward the horizon and streaks of sleepy blue are painted across the sky with a celestial paintbrush.

"Where are we?" I ask, though the question comes out more of a grunt.

Jade shoots me a look, her eyes sparkling. "So you can talk?" she quips with a faint smirk.

When I frown at her, she shrugs and pushes open her door. "I just thought you didn't like me," she sighs as she climbs out onto the grass.

I quickly haul myself out of the car and stride forward toward her, gently gripping her arm between my fingers. She flattens slightly against the car, her chest rising in shallow pants.

"Why would you think I didn't like you, eh?" I ask sternly.

I don't know what's come over me. I have this sudden, primal urge to make sure Jade knows that

I've never not liked her. That's bloody incomprehensible.

"I..." she drags in a shallow breath. "It's just that you can never be bothered to look at me. You never talk to me either. I just assumed..."

I release her, taking in the way her plump mouth purses. Her chest rises and falls, her full breasts straining against her top. I grit my teeth, the heat of her flesh lingering under my palms.

If I don't let go of her now, I may never.

Pushing away from Jade, I take a step away toward the trail nearby.

She stands still next to the car, her gaze blistering against my back.

Even though I know I should bite my tongue, my heart is pounding from being so close to her for the first time.

Without looking at her, I quietly growl, "Believe me when I say you have that all wrong."

## CHAPTER FOUR

# Jade

My heart is in my throat as Kai walks away from me. When he steps between the trees, the fading sunlight dapples across his striped rugby jersey.

Jolts of electricity still travel through my arm where he'd only just been touching me.

What did Kai's words mean?

What am I supposed to believe – what he says or how he acts? There's such a stark contrast between the two.

Swallowing hard, I rush after Kai between the trees. He doesn't know where he's going and he's going to need me to guide him before we both end up lost out here.

I rush forward a little faster, but it's a struggle to keep up with his long stride. He towers over my head, making me feel safe even as we head further away from the road. The trail is worn but faint. I reckon my brother and I are the only ones to ever use it in some time.

"Did I hear you say something about a nursing program?" he asks, still pacing in front of me. His strong footstep snaps a twig beneath his muscled body.

I nod, then realize he can't see me from behind him. "Yeah, no. I'm not sure about that anymore. Ryder doesn't seem too keen on it."

Kai pauses so abruptly that I almost tumble into his back. I manage to skid to a stop, gasping as Kai turns to gaze down at me.

"If that's your dream, you need to chase it. You can't let someone else define your destiny... and I think you'd be a great nurse."

My throat goes tight as I note the slight pain in Kai's eyes. Is he speaking from experience? Even though he and Ryder are close, I don't know much about Kai's personal life.

"Where are we going?" he then asks as if to change the subject, allowing me to finally move in front of him.

Am I imagining the way I feel his eyes drift over the length of my blue dress now?

"Here," I answer.

I gesture forward and we step between the trees, finding ourselves in front of a small, bubbling pond. A few birds squawk in the trees, the leaves rustling as stars peer curiously down at us. The water is clear and blue.

He looks around and then back at me, his head tilting curiously. "And where is here, exactly?"

I look at the pond, watching the lazy tide lap at the grassy bay.

"This is where Ryder and I go every year on the anniversary of our parents' passing," I whisper. "Or I reckon it's what we used to do every year. Ryder hasn't been here in..." Come to think of it, I can't remember the last time my big brother did make the trip out here with me. I clear my throat. "Our family used to come out here for picnics when we were kids and I just like to come here and remember them."

"I'm sorry he didn't come today," Kai offers. The sincerity in his warm voice is soothing.

I shrug. Despite the way Ryder and I bash heads and the way Ryder might come off immature, he looked after me when we lost our parents. He made sure I was always safe and warm and sheltered. I owe him a lot for that. There's a side to him that not many others get to see.

I know Ryder is moving on. He has his career to think about and his friends and the girls I'm not supposed to know about.

But me? I still feel like I'm picking up the pieces of my heart that shattered the day my parents never came home. That's why I need to be a nurse. The medical staff that tried to save my parents worked so hard, and even though they didn't succeed, I want to do what I can to help others in that same way. I just wish my brother would support me as I've always supported him.

When tears begin to brim in my eyes, Kai gives a fierce, protective growl unlike anything I've ever heard.

He moves suddenly, dwarfing me as he lunges closer to pull me into his arms. I gasp as he embraces me, crushing me against his hard, muscled chest. Against my cheek, I can feel his heart pounding. Intense heat more blistering than the New Zealand sun surges through me. My veins feel like they're boiling and something foreign coils tight in my core. My body seems to vibrate with every short breath I manage to take.

Slowly, I tip my head back to look up at Kai, but he's already gazing down at me with churning eyes of molten brown so dark it's nearly black.

Never before have I wanted anything like I want him to kiss me.

Before I can beg for even a single kiss, he dips me back slightly so that his mouth can capture mine.

The kiss is rough and tinged with a desperation that makes me weak in the knees. He grips my hips, his tongue brushing over my lips as I drink in his kiss.

I know this is wrong. I know if Ryder saw us now that he would be furious.

Though my big brother's name rises in the back of my mind, my desire for Kai quickly squashes it. Right now, all that matters is Kai. I'm finally in his arms where I belong and I never want this moment I've fantasized about for years to end.

"Jade..." he growls against my lips, his voice deep and raw with lust.

No one has ever said my name like that. I want to hear him say it over and over and over again.

He clutches me to him and I can feel his swollen desire throbbing in his tiny rugby shorts. I gasp in a short breath and circle my arms around his neck.

"I want you," he breathes.

Stars burst against the backs of my eyelids as my lashes flutter with raw desire. When I speak, my voice is breathless and faint, "Then have me."

## CHAPTER FIVE

# Kai

Seeing that sadness in Jade's eyes when she spoke about her past was more than I'd been able to handle. I'd needed to do something – anything – to bring some kind of light back to her typically radiant expression.

I understood Ryder's fear when it came to letting Jade bloom into adulthood, but what Ryder couldn't grasp was that Jade was already there. She'd already become a woman, and he was trying to prevent something impossible now. No amount of holding her back could protect her from the world.

As she sighs against my lips, her fingers knotting against my scalp when she runs her hands through my hair, primal desire ripples through me again and again.

I've wanted this moment to happen for so very long that I can hardly believe it's actually happening now. Here, beneath a dawning evening and twinkling stars and rustling trees, it feels almost magical.

We sink down together against the soft earth, cradled by warm leaves and fragrant soil. Patches of flowers reach up toward the evening sky, their scent sweet and subtle.

Hungrily kissing, we claw at one another's clothes, desperate to touch one another's bare flesh. I press Jade into the grass beneath me, feeling her body grind against my own. Every inch of her body that collides with mine causes sparks to fly. I wouldn't be surprised at all if this whole glen caught fire, the air between us has gotten so blisteringly hot.

When I pull her dress over her head and throw it aside, she tries to fold her arms in front of her, but I gently grasp her wrists and pull them to the side.

"I want to see you, all of you," I growl before kissing her again. I kiss down the side of her neck and then nip at her collarbone before kissing across her shoulder. My hands explore her, feeling her whole body.

I've never wanted anyone like this.

Her chest heaves as I kiss every inch of her that I can reach, and every time she exhales, the sound is more of a mewling moan. Her eyes roll back, the heat between her plump inner thighs radiating.

I can smell how much she wants me, and it makes my own desire climb.

"You're so fucking beautiful," I whisper.

The moon has now fully risen and its silver glow envelops her completely. Her hair is spread like a dark halo around her lovely face and her lips are swollen from kissing.

Her eyes, which are hooded and hazy from lust, focus on my face.

"But... if you think I'm beautiful... why didn't you ever talk to me?"

My back molars grind together and I lean down to press a kiss against her lips and then rest my forehead on hers.

"I wanted you too much to talk to your or even bloody look at you, Jade. I knew if I spent more than a second beside you, I'd be overcome with this need to feel you against me, to have you in my arms. The temptation was too great."

"Kai..." Her hands dance over my bare chest. Her fingers follow the inked paths of my tattoos. "The whole time, I wanted you too. I reckoned you could look at me like this. I never thought you'd want me."

I pin her against the ground and her legs twine around my waist.

Against her lips, I respond, "You're all I've ever wanted, Jade."

I capture her mouth again, our tongues wrestling. Her sweet flavor bursts against my lips. She tastes of strawberries and vanilla and something entirely unique to her. It's a flavor I can't get enough of.

My body screams for Jade, and the tip of my engorged, throbbing manhood presses between her thighs. The velvet lips of her womanhood greet me with slick heat and my eyes all but roll back in my head.

"You feel so bloody good," I moan against her lips.

I begin to thrust into her when she gives a cry, her fingernails digging into my back. I pause to look down at her with concern. Her face is contorted, and more tears have begun to leak from her eyes. I cup her face, kissing away each tear.

My body strains with restraint as I try not to keep thrusting. Was I being too rough with her? I'd been afraid of just that.

"What's wrong?" I ask huskily.

"I..." she whispers. "I've never... this is my first time..."

My throat tightens. "Wait, Jade... are you a virgin?"

She winces and bites her lips, squeezing her eyes shut for a long moment. That's enough of an answer for me.

"Why didn't you tell me, Jade? I could have tried to be more gentle... we don't have to do this-"

"I want to do this, Kai!" she interjects desperately. She clings to me, legs still wrapped around my waist. Her tears have slowed and pure longing shines from her blue eyes. "I didn't tell you because I didn't want you to worry about me - and I don't want you to be gentle! I just want you, all of you, as much as I can handle."

A primal, hungry growl of desire ripples through me as I slowly nod. I don't ask again if Jade is sure that she wants to do this, because I can tell just by her expression that she wants this as much as I do.

I'm glad she doesn't expect me to be gentle because I'm not even sure what that means – and right now, my body has had enough of restraint.

I press further into her, kissing her hard as she gives another quiet cry of pain. Her body strains to accommodate my swollen length. She clings to me, her cry melting into a moan as I bury myself inside of her. She pants, head falling back against the earth as I begin to move.

Our rhythm builds with fervent passion as each stroke becomes deeper and harder.

Being one with her is as close to heaven as I may ever get.

Suddenly, Jade cries out my name in a tone I've never heard coming from her mouth.

Her whole body shudders, her innermost muscles rippling and tightening around my manhood. It's too much for me to handle and I bury myself to the hilt within her one final time, my own cries of ecstasy twining with hers.

Again, we fall back into the soil, clinging to one another and kissing. I hold her to my chest, one arm around her plump waist as I stroke the hair back from her face.

If I never had to let go of Jade, I'd be the happiest man in the world.

Unfortunately, I know nothing is that simple, and I'm already dreading the next dawn that would rise without her in my arms.

## CHAPTER SIX

# Jade

Outside my bedroom window, a storm is brewing.

I lean my cheek against my palm, watching as dark clouds slowly creep across an equally dark sky. The heavy drops begin to tap loudly against the window before gliding down the glass the same way sweat glides down Kai's chiseled body.

As the sudden thought of the rugby player's naked, rugged figure, heat begins to simmer in my core.

Have weeks really flown by since Kai and I first got together?

That night by the pond is one that I'll never forget. I almost can't even remember what it felt before having known the flavor of his intoxicating kiss. It's as if we've already been together forever.

After that first enchanting evening, he and I weren't sure what to do. All that we did know is that keeping our distance from one another was impossible.

Touching him, kissing him, embracing him... it makes me feel whole in a way I've never experienced. According to him, he feels the exact same way.

I still can't believe that all this time, he's pined for me the same way I yearned for him.

Every moment spent with Kai feels like a fairytale... aside from the fact that my brother would feel completely betrayed if he knew what was happening behind his back.

I try not to think about that too much.

Behind me, Ryder tromps across the living room toward my room. When he appears in my doorway, he's dressed to go out again despite the storm. That's my big brother, he can never say no to a party. Tonight, I'm counting on just that.

"How ya going, Jade?" he asks curiously. "I reckon you've been staring out that window all day."

I push my hair back from my face and turn away from the storm beyond the windowpane. The sound of water striking the glass echoes faintly.

"I'm fine," I answer with a forced smile.

Ryder nods faintly and appraises me before sighing and sinking down on the corner of my bed. He fidgets, drumming his fingers against his knees as though he's nervous, but I'd never known Ryder to be anxious about anything.

"So..." he mutters, clearing his throat. "I know today was the day for you to apply to that nursing program. I reckon you might be a little sad that I talked you out of that whole mess..." He trails off, at a loss for words for perhaps the first time in his twenty-some years.

"It's nothing," I interject, forcing yet another smile. "Really. You go have a good time tonight, eh?"

"Straight up?" Ryder murmurs, frowning at me. He looks entirely unconvinced that I'm okay. His fingers are still tapping a concerned rhythm into his leg.

"Yep!" I answer, trying to sound like my bubbly self.

He nods and winks. "Don't do anything I wouldn't do," he teases before heading out the door.

When the front door of the flat swings shut, I heave a sigh so deep and heavy it probably came from my toes. I lean forward, shaking my head. I'd begun to think he was never going to leave.

I race over to the window, peering down onto the street as Ryder dashes toward his car. Our flat is nestled in the heart of Auckland, so we're not far from the nightlife, but when Ryder goes out, he goes all out. He'll be occupied for hours – if not the entire night.

This makes it the perfect opportunity for Kai and me to get some much needed alone time. Neither one of us likes being this underhanded, but it's for Ryder's own good.

A few moments later, another pair of headlights washes up the street as Kai's car pulls up to the curb a little ways from the flat. A faint squeal of excitement escapes me as I turn toward the front door. Any time apart felt like too much time apart, and every reunion was just as sweet as the first time he and I held one another.

When the door swings open, I spring right into Kai's waiting arms. He spins me, kissing me and embracing me tight against him. I sigh and melt into his chest, letting my greedy hands stroke up and down his body.

"How long do you think we have?" he asks as we sink down onto the couch.

When I move to sit beside him, he pulls me into his lap instead. I straddle him, allowing my hands to splay out over his muscled chest. I brush the tip of my nose against his before drinking in a long, sweet kiss that leaves me blinking away stars in my eyes.

"A few hours, at least," I answer.

He smiles, but it's tinged with bittersweet sadness. "And that won't be nearly long enough."

I nod in agreement. "But I'm glad you're here... Ryder brought up the nursing school program again and I just..." I trail off and lean down so that I can nestle my head in the crook of his neck. "I just worry I made the wrong decision."

"About applying when you told him you didn't?" he presses softly.

His strong fingers brush up and down my back as he holds me a little tighter against him, as though he could protect me from the pain of my own choices. I snuggle a little closer before nodding again.

"I hate lying to my brother. He and I have already been through so much over the years and he's always gone out of his way to protect me, even if his definition of trying to protect me borders on suffocating me at times. He's going to find out about the fact that I applied to uni even though he thinks it's not a good idea... and he's going to find out about us eventually too."

Kai tips up my face, his thumb brushing over my cheek as he gazes into my eyes.

"I'm not going to tell you that you're wrong, Jade, because you're not. Maybe it's time we come clean. I can be right by your side the whole time. I know how it feels to be stuck between what you want and what your family wants for you. It ain't bloody easy, that's for sure."

"What do you mean?" I press gently. "I want to know more about you, Kai. I want to know everything."

Over the past few weeks, Kai had hinted about his own past, but I'd yet to fully grasp what he'd been through. He was always so much more keen to focus on my issues, but I wanted to do what I could to support him too.

He frowns but continues stroking my cheek tenderly. For a man who was worried about being gentle, he always knows just how to touch me. I press my palm over his large hand, lacing my fingers with his.

"Please?" I prod softly.

His mouth screws one way and then the other, and then his eyes slowly lift to gaze into mine. I hold my breath as though I'm worried even the slightest sound will scare him off the topic again.

"My parents never wanted me to join the rugby team. They thought it was a waste of time and money. That I should go be a professor or something bloody boring like that. But I knew what I wanted... and that was rugby."

"So you told them that you'd made up your mind?"

He nods faintly, eyes glazing as his thoughts slip into the past. "And my father cut me out of his life. He said I'd disappointed him, and he wanted nothing to do with me after that."

I squeeze his hand. "Do you think that's what Ryder is going to do when he finds out about my nursing program and about us?"

Kai blinks and straightens slightly, his arms looping around my waist to hold me closer.

"No," he responds firmly. "There's not a damn chance that Ryder would ever push you away like that, Jade."

I cling to him, leaning against his chest. Kai makes it sound so straightforward and simple, but I'm not sure that's the reality of the situation.

But, even still, Kai is right.

I can't keep lying to my brother. I have to tell him the whole truth. Knowing that Kai is willing to stand at my side during that eases me slightly, but I know it'll be a rough conversation all the same.

"Let me make you feel a little better..." Kai whispers, pulling me closer.

I giggle as he lays me down against the couch, rotating his powerful body so that he's looming over me. I run my hands down his chest, marveling in how lovely it feels to be close to him.

"Kai..." I whisper, but he hushes me with a deep kiss.

I moan against his kiss, parting my lips so that his tongue can sweep over mine.

Outside the flat door, there's a sudden, sharp sound.

Before either of us can react, the door swings open.

"Jade," calls Ryder, "I reckoned you'd need some company and…"

My big brother trails off, taking in the sight of his best friend and I coiled together on the couch, my lips swollen and Kai pinning me against the cushions.

Ryder's jaw drops and pure fury fills his blue eyes.

## CHAPTER SEVEN

# Kai

"What. Is. Bloody. This?!" shouts Ryder. Each word that tears from between his gnashed teeth rises louder and louder with his anger.

Beneath me, Jade begins to tremble, tears instantly springing to her eyes. I lean back, pulling her upright so that she can fix her clothes. Then I scramble to my feet, making sure to stand between my best friend and his little sister.

I'm not worried that Ryder might do something to Jade. He wouldn't do anything to harm her, not physically at least. But I am worried that the raw rage on his face will scar her.

"Ryder... calm down, bro," I say quietly, but that only makes him howl with wrath.

"You're going to call me 'bro'?" he snarls. "After you took advantage of my little sister? You reckon I'm just going to be cool with that?"

"We were going to tell you!" cries Jade through her tears.

Ryder's blue eyes shift from me to her. Though his body goes slightly slack at the sight of her tears, I can tell he's still furious.

"How long has this been going on?" he asks, a vein throbbing in his forehead.

I step forward, moving again between Jade and Ryder. "Not long, and we really did mean to tell you."

Ryder's jaw again clenches and his fingers curl into fists. His whole body seems to be shaking.

"She's just a kid, Kai!" he yells furiously.

"I'm not a kid!" interjects Jade.

She pushes up from the couch and lurches forward to stand at my side. Ryder just gazes at her with wounded astonishment etched into his face. He hadn't expected her to stand up for herself.

"Jade..." Ryder murmurs, but Jade's heard enough.

As much as I want to push myself back between them, I know I have to let Jade speak for herself.

"I'm a woman, Ryder. I'm an adult. I have my own dreams, my own passions. Pretending I'm still a child isn't going to protect me from the world! I've grown up and I need you to accept that! There are things I want to share with you that I can't because you're so insistent on looking at me as young and naïve and innocent when I'm not anymore. I even applied to nursing school without telling you!"

"Why wouldn't you tell me that?" he cries.

"Because you didn't want to hear it! You didn't want me to live my life!"

Ryder swallows, his Adam's apple bobbing. His gaze swivels back toward me and, when his eyes lock on mine, his rage sparks anew.

"I just don't understand, Kai. She's my little sister. My only flesh and blood. How could you?!"

Before I can answer, Ryder has stormed across the room. He grabs me by the collar, dragging me closer. Jade shrieks and tries to stop Ryder, but I carefully push her back a step so she doesn't get caught in Ryder's rage.

This is between my best friend and me now. I've known this moment was coming from the second I first made the decision to kiss Jade.

"How could you?" Ryder repeats, shaking me. "You could've had anyone and I wouldn't have cared!"

"I didn't want just anyone!" I hiss back. "You always tease me about being your wingman because I never pick up any girls when we go out... it's because there's only ever been one girl that I've ever wanted, Ryder – and that's Jade! For as long as I can remember, she's been the one I feel like I can't live without. I've always tried to ignore those feelings, but it got to the point where I couldn't anymore!"

"What?" Ryder whispers, stunned.

He staggers back, releasing his hold on my shirt.

I move closer and put a hand on his shoulder, though he wrenches away.

"I love her, Ryder," I continue, voice thick in my throat. "I've loved her for so long that I can't remember a time before it. I've always wondered if pursuing rugby was the right choice because it put such a wedge in my family... but it brought me to her..." I pause, turning toward Jade.

She stands still, her hands on her cheeks, tears in her eyes as she gazes back at me.

"If rugby brought me to Jade," I continue softly, "then I know I'm on the right path. Any path is right as long as she's on it too."

"I love you too, Kai!" Jade whispers through her tears.

She stumbles toward me and I catch her, pulling her into my chest and pressing a kiss against her hair.

Then, slowly, I turn toward Ryder, still holding Jade as tightly as I could.

"You may not accept this... but I hope you will, Ryder," I state firmly, leaving no room for argument. I wouldn't let anyone get between Jade and me again. I'd spent far too long without her in my arms to let her slip away. "I love your sister, and I'll guard her heart and protect her spirit for the rest of my life if I'm so lucky."

Ryder's shoulders sag, but he slowly nods. He trudges over to us, laying one hand on my shoulder and the other on Jade's cheek. He looks warmly into his sister's eyes and then looks at me.

"I reckon you're right. I have no choice here. Jade is an adult and she can make her own choices... and I can tell by the way you speak that you do care about her, Kai. I've said this before, and I'll say it again... I know you'll take care of her."

I nod and smile at Ryder before embracing Jade a little tighter. She lifts her head so that she can gaze up into my eyes.

I rest my forehead against hers once more so that I can lose myself in her beautiful blue eyes.

Finding our way to one another hasn't been without struggle, but I know that fate is what led me straight into her arms. Jade is the love of my life and I intend on cherishing her forever.

# Jade

The pond gurgles quietly as I approach. The tall trees wave their long limbs back and forth as though I greeting me yet again. Smiling, I slide off my jandals so that I can let my toes dip into the cool water. Behind me, a few branches and leaves snap and rustle.

When I glance over my shoulder, Kai is standing there.

Instantly, my heart beats a little faster.

A slow grin spreads over his face as I turn and dart across the earth to leap into his arms. He holds me tight, pressing his lips against mine. I sigh against his lips, running my fingers through his hair. Every time I kiss him, it's better than the last.

We only part when another pair of footsteps join us on the dusty trail.

"I finally caught up with you lot!" says my brother cheerfully.

"Ryder, you came!" I gasp in surprise, turning to hug my big brother.

Ryder squeezes me and then claps Kai on the shoulder.

"I wouldn't miss it," he answers with a wink. "I'm done missing things. I decided to stop that the second I realized I'd missed the moment my little sister met the man of her dreams." He shoots Kai a playful look and the two men laugh.

A whole year has passed between that first time Kai and I truly connected.

Today, we gathered again at the pond to celebrate the memory of my parents. I'm so glad that both men in my life can be here, especially because I have something exciting to share.

"How's the move gone, bro?" Ryder asks Kai. "Did you find space for her shoes? Jade's got heaps."

It's my turn to laugh, though Kai slips an arm around my waist and squeezes me.

"It's been great," Kai says. "Spending time together every day has been amazing – overabundance of shoes or not."

I grin and nod along in agreement. Kai and I'd moved in together a few months back, and it truly has been wonderful. Between my difficult nursing program and his intense rugby schedule, crawling into bed together every night has been a blessing.

"I don't need too many bloody details," smirks Ryder.

To my brother's credit, he's done a great job accepting Kai and I as a couple. All three of us have become closer than ever.

"...I do have one little surprise since we're all here together," I begin slowly.

Ryder looks inquisitively at Kai, but Kai just shrugs, looking equally curious.

"I've been waiting for the perfect moment to announce this, but here in this special spot feels like it's just the right place..."

"Don't keep a bloke hanging, eh?" pouts Ryder. "Spill already!"

Kai laughs and nods. "What's going on, Jade?"

I bite my lip and then bounce up slightly on my toes. "I'm pregnant!" I cry, breathless with excitement and a little trepidation.

For a second, pure shock registers on the faces of both men. Then, as though they'd each been struck by lightning, they start to move.

"Pregnant?" gasps Ryder. "You mean my baby sister is having a baby?"

When I nod, Ryder starts jumping enthusiastically around the clearing. "A baby!" he shouts happily. "I'm going to be an uncle!"

Meanwhile, Kai sinks down to his knees in front of me, gently gripping my hips as he gazes at my face warmly and then my belly. He rests his cheek against my abdomen as though he could hear the little one growing inside. After a moment, he swallows hard and climbs to his feet. Behind us, Ryder is still energetically proclaiming his joy to the trees.

"Are you happy?" I ask softly.

Kai nods, collecting himself as he pulls me against him. He strokes my back and kisses me once more.

"I'm happier than I ever could've imagined," he says earnestly. "When I finally held you for the first time, I thought nothing could ever bring me more joy... but I was wrong. Right now, I'm so happy I could bloody explode. I love you, Jade, and I already love that little baby."

Happy tears form in my eyes as I lay my head on his shoulder. I close my eyes, heart so filled with love and joy that I could hardly stand it.

It's hard to believe that a year ago, Kai and I had yet to kiss or touch... and now, I get to kiss and touch him every day. Fate was kind the day it brought Kai and I together, and now my sexy rugby player and I get to spend the rest of our blissful days together.

The End

# MANU

## CHAPTER ONE

# Manu

The rugby ball launches into the air, making a satisfying *thunk... thunk... thunk* against my strong palms when I catch it.

With every forceful, upward thrust, the ball spirals perfectly. My aim remains high in the sky, like I'm trying to shoot it a little closer to the faint golden sphere peeking out from behind a thick grey haze.

A pair of studded cleats clomps toward me, but I don't look over. Instead, I catch the ball a final time before squatting slightly. The muscles of my toned and tanned legs strain while I expertly weave the ball between my calves.

"Manu!" Jax sighs. My teammate stands over me, blocking out what little sunlight shone in through the open roof of the TET stadium. "Why don't you try practicing with your team for once, eh? You've been doing solo drills all afternoon."

The ball is rough against my palms as I continue passing it around and between my legs. My body is screaming for a break, but with the first round of the National Cup in just a few days, I'm not about to go easy. Jax should appreciate that. He's the one whose all but obsessed with the sport. We all love the game, but he lives for it.

"...Manu? You listening to me, bro?" Jax prods irritably. "Or what, you can't be bothered today?"

I finally drop the ball and straighten up, my arms folding over my chest as I look straight into Jax's golden eyes.

"I reckon we'd be better with more action and less talking, don't you?" I grunt.

My chest heaves, damp jersey clinging to my body. I'm out of breath from the day's hard work out.

Jax's lips purse, probably because he knows I'm right. Afterall, we'd managed to secure just a few hours in the TET stadium to practice for our match against the Taranaki team in a few days. We need to make use of every second we have on the field. Even though we're away from home, some of the local Auckland fans here in New Plymouth had gotten wind of our practice and have crowded into the stadium to watch us do drills.

But apparently Jax is more interested in having some sort of bloody counseling session rather than keep playing.

"What's wrong with you?" he asks. He lifts a hand and shields the sun off his face. "You've been straight up crabby ever since the plane landed."

My back teeth clench hard together. "Don't know what you're on about. I'm good as gold, mate."

"That's a bloody yarn if I've ever heard one," smirks one of the other players. I shoot an aggravated look at Gray, who'd been watching Jax and I with keen interest. "When we got to the hotel yesterday, I could hear you stomping around even from my own room. Can't imagine how Kai got any sleep at all. I'm sure glad I didn't have to bunk with you."

"Piss off, Gray," I grumble.

This, naturally, only seems to amuse the other rugby player.

"Oi, why don't you just tell us what's going on?" Jax sighs. "I thought you'd be happy since we're back in your hometown."

My gritted teeth begin to grind. Being back home might've made someone else cheery, but not me. I've felt on edge ever since we arrived here. There'd been a time a long while back where I'd wanted to play for the Taranaki team... but in the end, I'd had to leave. I couldn't stay a second longer.

"Hey!" someone says, snatching the ball from me from when I lean down to grab it again.

Ryder's blue eyes burst into my vision. The dark-haired rugby player leans closer and pokes playfully at my chest. When I grab at the ball, he tosses it just out of my grasp. Like Gray, Ryder is mischievous and a little too loud – and today I'm in no mood to entertain him.

"Now that we're back in New Plymouth, you don't want to be part of our team anymore?" Ryder asks, pretending to pout. "Is that it?"

"Watch it," I hiss.

Ryder's grin widens as he continually maneuvers the ball just out of my reach. Every time I try to grab it and he darts it away, my irritation swells.

"Give me the bloody ball," I demand, looming over Ryder's dark-haired head just as another player wedges himself between us.

"Let's just calm down," instructs Kai. As usual, he's shirtless – if only just to show off his tattoos. "Jax, I reckon the pressure is getting to us lot. Time for a break, eh?"

Jax sighs, eyes skimming the field before he reluctantly nods. "Alright. Let's leave it for today. Most of us got a good practice in." He looks pointedly at me, but I just shrug. I got in a good practice too, just one on my own. "Everyone get some rest so we can resume our drills tomorrow. And keep in mind that we're here for Auckland. No one else."

I roll my eyes and look away, abruptly finding myself lost in a pair of familiar chestnut eyes that blaze directly into mine. As I take in the brown-haired beauty amidst the Auckland fans in the stands, my breath catches in my throat, my heart dropping like are rock all the way to my stomach.

Time might as well have screamed to a halt.

In that single instant, I forget the game and I forget my frustration... and I'm all too reminded why I left my hometown.

This time, I'm sure as hell not making the same mistake twice.

CHAPTER TWO

# Liv

Swirling grey cloud shift and churn in the distance as the whitecapped peak of Mount Taranaki pierces the haze, patiently allowing the clouds to dance around it. Even from the TET stadium stands, you can gaze out toward its colossal glory.

Usually, I'm astounded by the volcano's beauty even though I've spent my whole life in New Plymouth, but today I'm snared by a brilliant pair of ebony eyes instead.

Despite going to the stadium specifically to try and catch a glimpse of the sexy Samoan rugby player, it'd still stunned me to see him there when I pushed through the other Auckland fans to peek out onto the field.

It's so bizarre to me that the tiny, tan wild child that was young Manu grew into such a powerful beast of a man.

We'd been neighbors once upon a time, though that feels like another life entirely and so much has changed between then and now.

I reckon I've faded from his memory by this point. He probably doesn't recognize me at all.

How would he ever remember a pair of quiet brown eyes peeking over the fence to watch him practice rugby day in and day out? We were just children. He had his uninhibited love for his sport while I cherished my books and quiet flowers.

But the way Manu is looking at me now... is it because my face is niggling some distant memory in the back of his mind?

Either way, his intense dark-eyed gaze makes heat flutter along with the butterflies in my stomach. When we were teens, before he moved away to pursue rugby, I'd always longed for him to look at me just like this. Back then, I'd watch him practice exactly as I had today and wish that he would finally see me the way he saw his rugby dreams. It wasn't like I ever worked up the courage to talk to him. I was always far too timid.

Unfortunately for me, that is likely the only thing that hasn't changed between then and now.

The players begin to make their way off the field, signaling that their practice has finished for the afternoon. A few of them I recognize, but it's only Manu whose career I've really been following. The fans begin to slowly lumber away from the stands and I allow myself to be pulled along the tide of people flowing toward the exit.

I make my way out of the stadium, smiling faintly when I spot a rainbow of spring flowers blooming in the grass nearby. They don't seem to care that spring, so far, has been windy and cool. They're happy to blossom all the same. I wander over, wanting to pick some to take home with me, but in the end, I decide to leave them where they are so that their petals can bring happiness to someone else who passes by.

"Liv!" a voice calls from behind me. The sound of the familiar shout is enough to every hair on the back of my neck lift like I'd been struck by lightning.

I gasp shortly and whirl around to see Manu lumbering toward me. The rugby player is even taller and broader than I expected. His arms are practically thick as tree trunks and his body looms like Mount Taranaki over my head.

I muster up a smile, still startled by his sudden appearance. Can he hear my heart beating like crazy in my chest? The rapid pace is making me dizzy. I glance around, trying to make sure I'm not imagining him talking to me right now, but a few of the fans have stopped to snap pictures on the phones of the massive man.

"How ya going?" he asks, "All good, I reckon?"

Somehow, I manage to nod despite my dazed state.

"Manu... It's... um, it's so good to see you!" I answer, my voice breathless with surprise. "I can't believe you remember me after all this time."

Surprise registers on his own handsome face for a moment, as though I'd said something utterly ridiculous. For the life of me, I can't figure out why the statement would've caught him off guard.

He shifts and drags a hand through his hair. Though the sun is struggling to shine through the cloud cover, Manu's skin gleams with sweat and I can make out every chiseled muscle on his body with the way his jersey is clinging to his dark skin. It's enough to turn the fluttering butterflies in my stomach into a cyclone. I blink hard, trying to focus, but I just keep getting more lightheaded.

"I think we should catch up," continues Manu. "Tonight, eh? We can go out somewhere."

Again, my chin slowly dips up and down. Manu is asking me out. Is this really happening? Why?

Does he just need help reacquainting himself with New Plymouth?

Surely that's all this is.

It's only after Manu and I have exchanged numbers and he's retreated back to the other Auckland Rugby Union players that I realize he probably has no idea just how much my life has changed since last we spoke.

CHAPTER THREE

# Manu

"It was so crazy to see Liv, of all people, standing in the stands this afternoon. Like, I can't be bothered to believe in fate or anything bloody ridiculous like that, but Liv? Really?" I ramble as I run my hands through my hair and doublecheck how I look in the mirror.

If I'm about to catch up with the girl I crushed hard on all throughout my childhood, I'm going to look my damn best.

"..."

Sighing, I turn around to frown at one of the quieter members of our rugby team.

Kai just arches an eyebrow before simply responding, "Choice."

I smirk back at him. "Don't pretend like there's not some cute girl you've got your eye on that you'd rant on about like this too, eh?"

Kai hastily clears his throat. Is it my imagination or is he blushing?

He doesn't answer, choosing instead to look back at the notepad in his lap. Jax had asked him to make a list of drills for us to practice tomorrow. The dark-haired man is sprawled out on one of the two hotel beds in the room that he and I are sharing. Everyone on the team has been buddied up for the next couple of days while we awaited our big match against Taranaki.

"You think she would've mentioned it if she was seeing somebody?" I ask, stroking my chin and frowning.

It hadn't occurred to me that she and some bloke might be together – though I wouldn't be surprised if Liv had found somebody. She's beautiful and kind. Anyone would kill to be with a girl like that.

Oh, hell. It'd be bloody awkward if she brought somebody out with us. She hadn't been wearing a ring this afternoon, had she? Not one that I'd noticed anyway.

Abruptly, the door is thrown open without a knock. It swings, crashing loudly against the wall as Ryder and Gray both spill inside. Both of them carry a small case of beer. No doubt, they'd snuck it by Jax, who would be keeping a close eye on the hotel bar until after our match against the Taranaki team.

"What are you lot up to?" asks Gray jovially.

Ryder flops onto the corner of Kai's bed and holds out a beer. Kai grins, tossing aside his notepad and cracking open the can.

"Manu here is getting ready for a date," quips Kai, his eyes flashing.

Ryder gasps and leaps up. "Straight up? You're going out on the town and you didn't even ask me to come with you? That's bloody rude."

"It's not a date," I mutter. "I'm just seeing a girl I used to know."

"Mmhmm, heard that one before," Ryder mutters with a roll of his eyes. He playfully nudges Kai, who really is blushing now. "Just like Jade is just a girl you know, Kai?"

"This isn't about me," protests Kai despite the faint smirk dancing on his face.

Gray tilts his head back, finishing his beer and then tossing it aside. "Not everything is about women, boys. And at least you're looking a little more alive than you were earlier, Manu. A hot girl is all you needed to lift your spirits?"

"When is a hot girl not enough to lift someone's spirits?" sighs Ryder dramatically.

The group laughs, but I don't pay them any attention. My phone has buzzed in my back pocket and I'm now hastily fishing it free. When I see Liv's name pop up, I scroll through the message, quickly skimming the text.

*"Sorry, Manu, I can't go out... but you can come over if you'd like?"*

Below the message, Liv had included her address. I recognize it vaguely as a location near the New Plymouth beach a ways from where we'd grown up as neighbors.

If she wanted to be all alone at her house, I was more than down for a quiet night in.

"Cheers, boys, I'm out of here," I announce before pushing my way out of the now crowded hotel room.

With every step I take, my grin widens more and more.

I'd left New Plymouth to try and forget my feelings for Liv, but now I finally had a chance to have her all to myself.

## CHAPTER FOUR

# Liv

I blame the text inviting Manu to my place on the glass of nearly-finished red wine sitting on my kitchen table.

Drinking normally isn't my thing, but the thought of not getting to see my childhood friend tonight called for a bit of liquid courage to keep that ball rolling. Manu and I hadn't even been in the same city in years, and I wasn't about to miss a chance to talk to him for even a little bit.

I'm still sure that this will be nothing but a brief visit. Manu spotted me and must've felt suddenly homesick. We were simply two childhood neighbors getting together to chat about how New Plymouth has changed and how our lives have evolved.

At least I'll have a few big things to share, I observe with a wince.

For good measure, I take another hearty gulp when I realize my fingers are trembling. I don't know why I'm letting myself get so nervous. I had a crush on Manu when we were kids, but we're totally different people now. I'm sure that whatever spark I felt in the past must have extinguished a long time ago. And, even if embers of that spark still stubbornly flicker somewhere deep in my heart, that feeling certainly won't be reciprocated. Manu probably has women falling all over him back in Auckland – and all over New Zealand for that matter.

Tires crunch up my driveway, the sound of which causes a shiver to roll up my spine.

Footsteps slowly tread closer and I know Manu has arrived even before seeing him. I remember how I would hear him leaving his home next door before dawn so that he could get extra rugby practice before school. Every morning, I would half wake to the sound of him walking by my window.

I take a half-step toward the door, wondering if I should open it or allow him to knock. In the end, I wind up awkwardly hovering until a powerful knock resounds through the house.

Quickly, I pull open the door, greeting him with a shy, but bright smile.

"G'day, Liv," he murmurs.

He steps inside and closes the door, his dark eyes locked on me.

His arms open, welcoming me into a tight hug I'm all too eager to melt into.

I have to bite back a gasp as he squeezes me, overwhelmed by how strong and hard his body has become. I can't suppress the thought that he could crush me with ease if he wanted too. I feel so small and protected in his embrace.

When his hold on me begins to loosen, I have to give myself a rousing little shake to convince myself to release him as well.

"This is a nice place you've got," he says, stepping in and shedding his coat. Manu's eyes skim my small home and a smile brightens his handsome face. "Look at these flowers, Liv! They're beautiful!"

I glance around, smiling at the arrangements dotting my home. Bouquets and garlands that I'd created myself are everywhere.

"I work as a florist. I take home the extras whenever I can."

"A florist," he echoes, his eyes softening. "Fitting. You were always knee-deep in your little garden, dirt smudged on your face."

My cheeks sear pink. I'd never realized he saw me gardening.

"What about your husband? What does he do?" Manu asks.

I resist the urge to grimace, forcefully tucking a lock of brown hair behind the curve of my ear instead.

"Yeah, no... there's no husband in the picture."

Manu's brow lifts slightly but he makes no further remark, for which I'm grateful, though I wish I could have come up with some sort of response that would ease the sudden awkwardness rising between us.

We gaze at one another, not speaking. From the open windows of the home, the sound of the ocean lapping at the New Plymouth beach echoes faintly.

"Can I get you a drink?" I ask, pointing toward the open bottle of red wine on one of my counters.

"That would great..." he starts to say, trailing off as his jaw drops. He blinks hard, stepping closer to look at the photo beside the bottle of wine.

From the glossy photo, I beam out toward the viewer, head slightly thrown back in silent laughter. But I doubt that's what he's looking at... it's probably the giggling four-year-old little girl snuggled in my arms that's caught him off guard.

"Ah... um... the reason I couldn't go out tonight, Manu," I say hesitantly, "is because I couldn't find a babysitter for my daughter."

CHAPTER FIVE

# Manu

It isn't the fact that Liv is a mum that shocked me.

Liv, tender and gentle and sweet Liv, surely was put on this world in part to become a mother. No, it was how much joy radiated from that single picture that captivated me. Throughout our youth, I'd seen her laugh and smile heaps, but never quite with the gusto she had in that picture.

I reckon that little girl must be Liv's absolute mini-me. Judging by the vibrant smile on the kid's face and the cozy feel to Liv's little home, Liv is as good of a mum as I would expect.

For a moment, I glance over the rest of the pictures hung on Liv's walls and on her shelves. They're all either of Liv and the little girl or of the little girl alone. Not one has anyone else caught in the frame.

When I turn my attention back to Liv, she seems to already know the question on my mind.

"Her dad left me when I was pregnant," she states quietly. Though her voice is soft, it's firm with a strength I'm not sure even Liv herself can hear. "Good bloody riddance too. We're better off for it. I just wish my own mum was still around. She'd have loved Rosie..." Her eyes fill with sadness, but her chin remains lifted.

A desire to protect her so intense that it flares my nostrils surges through me, but I stay silent so I can hear her quiet voice continue on a little longer.

"It's been hard going at it alone, but I take it one day at a time, you know?" she sighs.

"Liv..." I start to say, reaching out to touch her arm to comfort her. My fingers only just blaze a trail down her soft flesh when there's a shrill but tiny shriek from a nearby hall.

When I look toward the sound, a pair of wide chestnut eyes stare back at me.

The four-year-old from the photo clutches a teddy bear under one little arm, a lavender nightgown fluttering against the floor. Her cheeks are pink and pudgy.

"Mummy!" wails the girl. Her voice is as adorably sweet as her face. "Who is that? Was he banging on the door?"

"It's alright, sweetheart," Liv says hurriedly. "This is Manu! A friend!"

The little girl just hugs her teddy bear, frowning uncertainly at me.

I bend down, making sure each of my movements is slow and steady and that I'm keeping my distance from the little one, and wave at her. I'm perfectly aware of my stature. If I can intimidate other rugby players, I'm probably a beast to a tiny human like Rosie.

"My name is Manu," I explain gently. "I knew your mummy when we were as little as you are now! What's your name?"

"You used to be little like me?" the kid gasps.

Her fear melts, replaced instead by astonishment. She looks at Liv, who giggles and nods. Then the little girl looks back at me and toddles a little step closer.

"I'm Rose. This is Mr. Fluff," she adds, gesturing toward the teddy in her tight grasp. Mr. Fluff is old, his fur faded from lots of love over the last four years.

"Hello, Rose," I say with a little bow of my head before reaching out to shake her hand and then Mr. Fluff's battered paw. "It's very nice to meet both of you."

The little girl giggles and hides behind her teddy bear.

"Come on, Rosie," Liv says with a wink. "It's time you head back to bed. Say goodnight to Manu!"

Rose pulls away from her mom, rushing back over to me.

"Can you tuck me in?" she pleads. "You can scare away the monsters! You're bigger than all of them!"

I look at Liv, who grins and shrugs. Then, I stand back up and lead Rose back to her room. Her room is small but cozy and full of dolls and stuffed animals and clumsily drawn pictures. I tuck her snugly in then check for monsters under her bed and in her closet for good measure.

"Goodnight, Manu!" she calls. "Goodnight, Mummy!" Her voice is already drowsily fading, and by the time Liv and I have sidestepped the strewn about toys to escape into the hall and close the door behind us, Rose is snoring softly.

"Thank you for that, Manu," says Liv once we're back in the living room. "Rosie's a hard sleeper, she doesn't normally wake up once she's tucked in. She's usually a little shyer than that too. She must like you."

I chuckle faintly and shrug. "It was nothing. I always imagined myself being a dad by now. I've had to settle for being the favorite uncle instead, so I've gotten some practice here and there. You know, she seems like a sweet kid. I reckon you're doing a great job, Liv."

Liv looks up at me, a faint smile on her pink lips. "That's kind of you to say. It's hard to know if I'm doing things right. Am I making good choices for her? Am I setting a good example? I'm always wondering..." She shakes her head, suddenly seeming exhausted.

She leans against the wall, letting her forehead brush the plaster, and I can't resist the urge to reach out and comfortingly press my hand against her arm.

She inhales sharply when my flesh meets hers, and I can't help but wonder if she feels the same magnetic pull I do.

"I know years have passed since you and I have been neighbors, Liv, but I also know what a great mum you must be. Don't doubt that for a second."

Her eyelashes flutter as she gazes at me, the electricity between us crackling so loudly in my ears that I could've sworn a thunderstorm was blowing in from the beach. I take a step closer to her, my fingers slowly sliding down her arm.

Just when my fingers brush hers, she lurches away.

"How about we take a breather?" she whispers, turning to escape toward her patio.

Every step away she takes leaves my heart throbbing.

## CHAPTER SIX

# Liv

Pushing open the back door of my home, I hurl myself out onto the patio overlooking the beach. A rush of cold wind blows in off the sea. Its frigid fingers lifts my hair off my face but does little to soothe the heat boiling in my veins.

Since I can remember, I'd yearned for Manu, but he'd only ever seen me as the girl next door. Hadn't he? I'd tried everything to move on from him after he left to go to Auckland, including throwing myself into other relationships, but he'd always remained there in the back of my mind.

I suddenly feel his warmth behind me, rolling over me the same way the tide rolled in on the soft sand.

"Liv..." he says quietly, and even just that sends a shiver down my spine.

I've been alone for so long that I don't even remember what it feels like to have a man in my home... or in my bed.

Scorching hot desire blisters through my body. I'm glad I'm facing away from him now because he'd be able to see lust written all over my face. But am I even allowed to want Manu like this? I am a mother, but am I allowed to be a woman as well?

I don't know what to do, what to think. All I know is that I want Manu. I've wanted him for years.

He shifts, his hand extending toward me. His fingers slowly brush over my back, following the notches of my spine. My knees grow weak, my head foggy as the beach before me. Though the day had been cloudy, the night sky is clear and stars glisten in the ocean's reflection.

"I was so surprised to see you at the stadium today," he whispers.

I turn around, only to find that his eyes are churning too. I'm enraptured by the way the moon reflects in his dark irises.

"Why?" I ask.

He blinks, looking away for just a moment to organize his thoughts. Then, slowly, his gaze pierces mine again.

"Because you were the reason I chose Auckland over Taranaki."

His words hit me so hard that I stagger back a step, my back bumping hard against the rail of my patio.

"Why?" I repeat feebly. "I don't understand. I was just your neighbor. How could I have affected you at all?"

Manu eases forward toward me and my head tips back so that I can continue looking up into his face.

"Because to me, you weren't just the girl next door, Liv. You were the only girl I wanted. I never thought you noticed me. I played as hard at rugby as I did because I was hoping to impress you. When it became clear that wasn't going to happen... I knew I had to leave."

My chest heaves as I try to process his words. It's almost more than I can handle.

"Why didn't you ever say anything?" I cry out, frustrated. "I wanted you too, Manu! We could've..." I trail off, panting from the surprise of everything he's said. "So much time has passed!"

"I'm saying something now," he answers simply, though his voice has become deep and husky.

We stare at one another, my chest heaving and Manu unmoving. Then, Manu lifts one of his hands, his calloused fingers brushing my cheek. In that moment, I can no longer restrain myself.

All of my pent-up desire for Manu, all the time I've spent dreaming and longing for him, it all surges through me at once. I lean closer, grasping at his shirt. In that single moment, Manu too springs to life. He scoops me into his arms, his lips crashing against mine.

I moan into the kiss, allowing him to lift my body and slide me up onto the thick railing of the patio. The beach is still tonight and there will be no one to see us but the man on the moon. He leans me slightly backward over the railing, but I'm perfectly safe in his arms.

Kissing Manu is even more blissfully wonderful than I expected. Bolts of wild electricity leap from every one of my pores as he clutches me to his toned chest. His tongue ravishes mine, leaving me panting and pleading for more.

Heat explodes inside of me as I claw at his shirt, wrenching it over his head. He thrusts up my skirt, freeing my legs to wrap around his waist.

I can feel the hardened, throbbing length of his desire pulsing between my inner thighs, and it's enough to make my eyes roll back in my head. I cling to him, whispering his name over and over again just as I'd imagined it. One of his rough hands grips my ass, edging me closer to him so that the head of his manhood can slowly bury itself inside of me, while his other hand knots at the base of my knock. He tips my head back, kissing the sides of my neck. His teeth graze over my collarbone, his tongue dancing across my flesh.

I cry out with pleasure, the sound swallowed by the sea.

He thrusts deep within me, each strong stroke flinging me closer and closer to the edge of climax. All I can do is cling to him, my whole body wrapped around him, as pleasure explodes inside of me again and again. Red stars flare on the backs of my eyelids when he kisses my jaw, moaning my own name.

Over the roof of my house, I can see Mount Taranaki rising in the distance, but I close my eyes to block out the view.

I know this night will over far too soon, just as I know Manu will be back on the plane soaring away from me. But for now, I will hold onto him as tightly as I can.

## CHAPTER SEVEN

# Manu

The TET stadium is alive with activity. Fans are packed from edge to edge of the stands, each one decked out in Auckland or Taranaki gear.

As the few remaining seconds left in the game dwindle, cheers echo with deafening noise as the fans from each team trying to drown out the other.

Despite the cool weather, it's been an intense game and we're all drenched in sweat.

Again and again, we race across the field, hurling the ball to one another with laser-like accuracy and trying to tackle the opposing players.

Whenever possible, I spare a look toward the crowd – though I don't have to look very long. It's as easy to find Liv amongst the throngs of Auckland fans as it is to spot a moonbeam in a dark night.

She's glowing, waving at me and cheering. The past few days, when not practicing with the team, I've been with her. The nights have been full of passion, the mornings full of sweet moments, the afternoons full of playdates with Rosie. That little girl reminds me so much of Liv. She's joyful and bright and sweet, though not without a flair of impishness. Liv wanted to keep our romance a secret from Rosie, which I understood completely, but that hadn't stopped Rosie from demanding that we act out a wedding one day. It hadn't been a wedding between Liv and I, but between myself and Mr. Fluff, but it was fun all the same.

As I lift a hand to wave back at Liv, a body suddenly collides with mine. I stagger back, caught off guard. When I shoot a look toward the referee, he doesn't seem to be paying any attention. Bloody figures.

"What the hell?" I shout at the Taranaki player. "You wanna hiding or something?"

The other player grins at me, mouth twisting.

"Oi, Manu! I've heard about you! You weren't cut out for our team, so you ran off like a little teary-eyed boy to Auckland, eh?"

"Oh, piss off!" I hiss with a scowl.

"You want to be on our team so bad you're even trying to get with one of our local babes, right? I bet she's a real filthy girl to be with the likes of you-"

Fury suddenly fills me as the Taranaki player brings up Liv. After all that she's been through, I'm not going to let anyone bad mouth her. She's too good for that.

"You leave her out of this!" I roar, rushing at him and shoving him back.

A whistle blares as the referee throws a red card onto the field.

"Get him off the field!" shouts the ref, but I don't hear him. All I see is the player mocking me.

"She'll come to her senses soon enough," the Taranaki player continues, still grinning widely. "Your team is rubbish – and so are you, Manu. Over thirty and not even on the Blues."

My fists clench. "I see what this is about now," I snarl. "You know we're about to kick your asses on the field so you're trying to distract me. You're the pathetic one, not me!"

The grin on the opposing player's face instantly fades, only to be replaced with raw rage.

He rushes toward me, fist pulled back. His fist flies through the air on a direct collision course with my jaw, but I manage to sidestep it just in time. I lunge at him instead, throwing him backward. He tumbles to the ground, chest heaving as he glowers up at me.

"I said get him off the field!" shouts the ref.

Gray suddenly grabs me, hauling me back and pushing me toward the sin bin.

"Take a breather or else you're going to end up costing us this win!" he whispers in my ear. "We've got seconds left, bro!"

I take one lurching step toward the penalty box, turning my head back toward Liv.

But Liv has stopped cheering. She's just staring at me, her eyes narrowed, her arms hanging at her side.

Just as Jax shoots a goal kick and the crowd goes wild, Liv turns and flees the stadium. Trapped in the sin bin, I'm helpless to go after her.

Even as our fans erupt with victorious cheers, my heart wrenches with pain.

CHAPTER EIGHT

# Liv

Tears blur my eyes as I park my car just outside my house. I grip the steering wheel, my chest heaving. My eyes squeeze shut as I try to pull myself together.

I can't let Rose see me so upset. She'll notice my red-rimmed eyes right away. She's too young to understand the thoughts whirling through my head and I'm not sure how to explain it all to her anyway.

Unfortunately, I also know I can't just hide outside my house all day. Rosie will notice my car at a point likely sooner than later. Sniffling, I push open the door and slowly step outside before making my way into the house.

"Oh, you're back early!" says the startled babysitter. "Rose is napping, but she should be waking up any minute now."

"Yes, thanks, you can go now," I answer, thrusting a few bills into her palm.

When the babysitter leaves, I sink down at the table and rub my hands over my eyes.

The events of the game continue to play in a loop in my head.

Manu's temper, the cheers of the fans as Auckland won the first round of the National Cup, the look on his face when that Taranaki player was taunting him... what am I to make of that? And what was I thinking getting involved with someone who lives so far away?

"Mummy?" whispers a little voice.

I look up in time to see Rose beaming sleepily at me. Her brown hair is pulled up in mussed pigtails and her eyes are still bleary from her nap. She rushes forward, climbing up into my lap. I wrap my arms around her and hold her close.

"Did Manu play good?" she asks in her sweet, tiny voice.

She perks up her head so that she can gaze curiously up at me.

"Of course," I answer, straining to smile back at her.

She inspects my expression, her own smile fading slowly. It was so easy to forget how adept children are at picking up emotions. I try to smile a little brighter, but it doesn't seem to convince my daughter.

"Then why are you back early?" she presses. "I heard the sitter say so!"

I playfully pinch one of her cheeks. "Because I missed you heaps and heaps!"

She giggles and hugs me tightly, distracted from her confusion over the expression on my face.

Relief rolls through me and I hug her to my chest, her head nestled against my shoulder.

"Is Manu going to come to play again tonight?" she asks, weaving her fingers into my hair. "I drew him a special picture."

Tears again threaten my eyes, but at least Rose is pressed against my chest. I hug her even tighter, biting my lip hard. Eventually, I inhale a shallow breath.

"You know, Rosie... Manu lives far away. He has to go back to his own house. I don't think he'll be able to play with us anymore."

Rosie gasps and lurches back. She stares at me, tears welling in the corners of her eyes. I stare back at her, heart breaking in my chest. How could I have allowed him into our lives when I knew he had to leave?

"But, Mummy, he's so fun to play with! He scares away the monsters!" wails Rosie. "I want him to come back! Make him come back so I can give him his picture!"

I don't answer. There's nothing I can say that will make sense to her or will ease her pain in any way. Instead, I pull her against me and cradle her tight. She continues to wail, her tears dampening my shirt as my own tears roll down my face.

I want Manu to come back too... but it's time I accept that he and I were never meant to be.

Just as a fence had separated our two backyards, miles of distance will continue to separate us forever.

CHAPTER NINE

# Manu

"Shots all around!" proclaims Jax, his words already beginning to slur together.

We'd been at the hotel lobby for hours and it was certainly showing. Kai and Ryder have their arms around one another, clinking their beer mugs together while drunkenly arguing about which of them scored the most points during the game. Ryder's trademark raucous laugh echoes through the hotel every few moments.

I just stare down into the bottom of my own untouched glass, watching as tiny bubbles float up from the bottom of the amber liquid.

"Back to being grumpy Manu, eh?" chuckles Gray as he slides into the seat beside me at the bar.

I just shrug, feeling far too worn out emotionally to be excited that we'd just won the first game of the cup. Judging by the rest of the team's enthusiasm, I'm not putting a damper on their party.

"I saw her," Gray continues, "the girl who was cheering you on. Is that the one you were going to see the other night? Is she the one you've been sneaking off to visit too?"

"Don't know what you're going on about, bro. It didn't affect my game," I grunt, finally taking a swig of my now room temperature beer.

"You're all good, bro," he shrugs. "I'm just wondering why you're not with her now."

"I reckon she doesn't want to see me." My fingers drum a disheartened beat against the smooth counter of the bar.

I don't know what made Liv run off like she had, but judging from the look on her face, she wanted nothing to do with me.

Jax suddenly thrusts two shots in front of Gray and me.

"Drink up, boys!" he demands exuberantly.

If I was feeling any more chipper, I would've found this hilarious. Jax is usually so tightly wound that he doesn't enjoy himself.

The rest of the team downs their shots and when I make no move to do mine, Gray does it for me. He smacks his lips, grinning at me.

"I may not look it, but I'm a smart bloke, Manu. I can tell you're all worked up about this girl. I can tell that's why you were off your game when we first got here. You're going to regret it if you don't go see her one last time."

While downing another slightly stale swig of my beer, I contemplate Gray's words. He has a point, I reckon. I'd dreaded coming to New Plymouth because the thought of Liv living a happy life with a happy husband just outside my reach killed me... and now that I'd arrived and found out that she wasn't in a relationship like I'd assumed she would be, I'd be making a huge mistake if I just let her slip away.

I'd done that once when we were younger, and I'd regretted it ever since.

"You're right, Gray," I announce, pushing back from the counter and smirking at him.

His steel-hued eyes brighten. "About going to see her?"

"That you're smarter than you look." I wink at him, playfully cuffing his shoulder before heading toward the hotel lobby.

With any luck, I'd have a reason besides our victory to celebrate tonight.

## CHAPTER TEN

# Liv

"Two whole scoops of ice cream?" cries Rosie out in pure, unadulterated delight. She stares down at her bowl, mesmerized by the big, rainbow-sprinkled globs.

Because it'd been a rough day, I'd decided there'd be no better dinner than dessert. Rosie, apparently, was in full-hearted agreement. A few hours had passed since Manu's rugby game finished, and night had fallen in New Plymouth.

Even though my heart is heavy, I can't resist a smile as I listen to Rosie giggling. I hope my little girl has a billion more moments just like this as she's growing up, where she's so overwhelmed by pure joy that she can hardly move.

That's how I felt waking up with Manu each morning...

I wince at the intrusive thought and shake my head. For all I know, he could already be on a plane back to Auckland right now. I don't know how long they were planning on staying in New Plymouth after their match, but it couldn't be long. They'd have to start prepping for their next game.

"Mummy..." Rosie murmurs, laying her hand on mine. She frowns up at me, little face slightly pinched. "Do you not like your ice cream?"

"of course I do!" I promise her, kissing her little cheeks.

"...Are you sad that Manu can't come play anymore?" she asks, pulling slightly back.

I sigh and then nod. It's no use trying to hide it from her. She'd long picked up on my feelings anyhow.

"Me too," she murmurs, picking up her spoon and digging it into her ice cream. She swirls a few sprinkles around, watching them leave behind a colorful streak in the vanilla scoops. "I liked him, Mummy. He was so big and so fun and so nice."

I laugh feebly and nod. "He was pretty fun, wasn't he?"

Again Rose nods. This time, she lifts her spoon and happily takes a bite.

Suddenly, she pauses, her head turning toward the door. "Did you hear that, Mummy? I think someone's here!"

As I'm pushing back from the table, someone knocks on the door.

Rosie excitedly rushes to the door, but I gently push her back. My heart throbs in my throat. I already know who's there. It's Manu. It has to be.

"I'm going to see who it is. You finish your ice cream, okay?" I direct Rosie.

She pouts but nods and retreats to the table. When she's distracted, I slip slowly outside.

As I slink out and carefully close the door behind me, my body brushes against Manu's. I inhale sharply through my nose, wishing that even just that slight touch wasn't enough to make my head spin.

"Manu, you shouldn't be here-"

"I'm sorry," he interjects softly. "I'm sorry that you saw me lose my temper on the field. That guy... I shouldn't have let him get to me."

I sigh and shake my head, nervously tucking my hair behind my ear. When a lock falls free, Manu instinctively reaches up to brush off my forehead. I bite my lip hard when his hand brushes my face, my knees going weak.

I lower my eyes, watching the way our shadows shift in the still night. "That wasn't the problem, Manu. Punch ups happen in rugby."

"Then what's wrong, Liv?" he asks, moving closer. "Why'd you rush out of the game like you did?"

He takes my hands in his, grasping them against his chest. I can feel his heart pulsing against my palms and I'm drawn closer to him even though I know it's only going to hurt me even more.

"You have to leave!" I whisper, voice breaking.

Manu's eyes pour into mine. His voice is thick and deep but sincere. "I'm not going anywhere until we talk."

"No... Manu... I mean that you have to leave – that's the problem! I live here, you live in Auckland. We can't be together! It hurts too much..."

His grasp tightens on my hands as tears pool in my eyes. He shakes his head, cupping my face.

"Then let's close the distance, Liv. I'll quit the team. I'll move back home to New Plymouth. I'll be here with you."

"Manu!" I gasp, but his eyes churn with fierce earnestness.

"I want you, Liv. I've spent my whole life wanting you and thinking I could never have you. Now, I'm willing to do anything so that I never have to say goodbye again. I love you. I've loved you longer than I can even remember. I've loved you since the first day I helped you dig for worms in your garden, since the first time you and I walked home from school, from the first time you said my bloody name. Nothing in this world means more to me than that."

The tears in my eyes spill down my cheeks and Manu pulls me against him, kissing each one away. I throw my arms around him and hang on tight.

"What do you say?" he murmurs in my ear. "We can take it as slowly as we need for little Rosie, but I'm not leaving you again."

"I say yes," I cry back, my tears turning to ones of joy. "Yes, Manu, yes. I love you too, but you can't quit rugby. I know how much you adore it. I'll move to Auckland. My family is gone and my flower shop can be moved. Rosie will love Auckland."

He leans his head against mine, his nose brushing mine. "Once we've won the National Cup, we can start planning."

"Oh, once you've won?" I laugh. "Someone's confident."

"How can I not be? I have the woman of my dreams in my arms?"

When I dissolve into laughter, happy tears still pouring down my face, the door cracks open.

"Manu!" cries Rose. "You came to play! Mummy said you had to go far away, but I don't want you to go!"

Manu leans down and Rosie leaps into his arms, wrapping him up in a big tight hug. He straightens back up and she continues to hold onto him.

"Mummy is always so happy when you're here, Manu! She smiles brighter than the sun!"

"Does she?" he asks playfully, winking at me. "Then I guess I can't go anywhere soon."

My cheeks glow bright red.

"That's right!" beams Rosie.

"He can go win Auckland a big trophy, can't he?" I ask Rosie.

She bites her lip, contemplating this while clinging to Manu, before reluctantly nodding.

"I guess... but you have to come right back!" she declares with a sigh.

Manu pulls us both into his arms, kissing Rosie's forehead and then my own.

"Don't you worry," he promises the both of us, "I don't plan on ever going far for long. My heart wouldn't let me."

# Manu

Atop my shoulders, Rosie's little body sways slightly back and forth as the three of us make our way toward our new home.

"What do you think?" I ask, tilting my head slightly up so that I can steal a peek at the four-year-old's face.

"It's so big! It's big like you, Manu!" she squeals. "We get to live here together?"

"That's right!" answers Liv. "We'll be one happy family."

Rosie kicks her legs slightly out of glee, but I make sure to have a steady hold on her with one arm while my other remains tight around Liv.

The last six months had been nothing short of wonderful. Once the National Cup was behind the team, I could focus on Rose and Liv and building a foundation for this very moment. I traveled constantly from Auckland to New Plymouth and we took our time introducing our relationship to Rosie. By the time we told the little girl that she and her mother would be moving to Auckland to live with me, she was elated. She demanded to start packing that very instant.

Now, I can hardly believe that we're here together and ready to start our forever.

We ride up the elevator to the apartment unit, a spacious one where Rosie would have plenty of room to thrive, but when I move to unlock the door, I find it's already open.

Liv frowns up at me worriedly, and I pass Rosie to her mother so that I can carefully push open the door and look inside.

The moment the door opens, the lights flash on.

"Surprise!" shouts the cluster of people inside.

The members of my rugby team excitedly jump around, greeting us.

"What the hell?" I ask, laughing as I help Rosie and Liv into the apartment.

The team rushes forward, grinning at me and patting me on the shoulder.

"When we heard Manu was bringing home a lady, we knew we had to welcome you," explains Ryder with a big grin. He looks at Liv and winks. "Welcome to the family, babe. Cheers!"

Happiness radiates across Liv's face as she laughs and nods. "Thank you! Thank all of you. This is so sweet."

Gray bends down in front of Rosie, giving her a high five as she giggles and says, "You lot are big like Manu! You all can scare away the monster from under my bed!"

I wrap my arms around Liv, pressing a kiss against her forehead and then her lips. She smiles up at me, snuggling deeper into my embrace while Jax and Kai give Rose a tour of her new home and tell her all about rugby.

"This is everything I've ever wanted," Liv whispers. "You're everything I've ever wanted, Manu."

I gaze back down at her, kissing her again. The kiss lingers, sweet and tender.

"And you and Rosie are my entire world. No matter how many trophies I may win, you two are my most valuable prize."


The End

# GRAY

## CHAPTER ONE

# Gray

I grit my teeth and charge forward, begging my legs to keep moving for the fifteen seconds left of the drill even though my muscles are screaming.

Coach's whistle blows sharply, piercing through the sound of the other rugby players grunting and wheezing. We've been dashing back and forth across the field, weaving between one another as we pass the rugby ball between us, for hours straight.

Our training was supposed to end earlier this afternoon, but now evening is swiftly falling. A cool wind blows as stars just barely begin to sparkle. This practice had been an especially intense one. With the final round of the National Cup looming, we all want to be in peak condition for the big game.

Finally, Coach's whistle blows one last time, signaling the end to the drill.

"I reckon you're bloody trying to kill me, Coach!" wails Ryder as he collapses dramatically against the soft earth.

Jax breathlessly chuckles from where he stands. His broad body is hunched, his hands on his knees as he gulps in shallow breaths of air like a man in the desert might gulp down water.

"I'm just trying to keep you lot in shape!" says the coach before he checks his watch with a wince. "Alright. I've got a conference call with the union that I'm about to miss. You blokes get some shut eye. See you bright and early!"

"Thanks, Coach!" calls Kai as the burly coach of the Auckland team turns and marches across the field towards an office tucked away near the stands.

"Suck up," Ryder mutters with a roll of his eyes.

Kai just smirks back at his best friend.

A rough hand claps at my shoulder as a chiseled, Samoan player ambles past me. Though my strong legs feel like jelly, Manu looks perfectly content. It's like he's barely even broken a sweat.

"How ya going, newbie?" Ryder calls over to me from where he's still sprawled in the grass. "All good?"

A short laugh escapes my throat. "I've been with the team for almost two years, bro. I don't reckon I'm a newbie anymore."

Ryder just laughs. He slowly pushes himself back up to his feet and stretches back and forth.

"Good thing I don't have any plans tonight with the ladies," Ryder grunts while lifting one arm over his head and bending to the side. "I don't think I'd be able to perform if you know what I mean."

"Seriously, Ryder?" groans Jax. "Think about the game for once instead of women."

I can't help but laugh. "Hah! That's like telling a cheetah to change its spots, bro."

Ryder turns toward me, his blue eyes playfully gleaming.

"Gray, you got something to say?" he says mischievously.

He launches at me, tackling me and wrestling me to the ground. We roll across the grass, trying to pin one another in a headlock. I've almost trapped

Ryder when someone grabs the back of my damp jersey and hauls me back to my feet.

Tall and tan Manu towers over us, smirking. "Oi! No one can get injured before the Cup, eh?"

"You got lucky this time," Ryder teasingly shouts at me.

When I nudge Ryder again in the ribs, we almost start roughhousing again before Kai throws his arms around both our necks to keep us apart. I grin, laughing and shaking my head back and forth. I might be one of the newest guys on the team, but I've loved every minute of it. They're like family to me.

I can't remember the last time I felt like I could truly trust anyone, especially not after what happened last year. These blokes and this game were the only things keeping my head on straight.

I wouldn't trade it for anything. This lot may not be blood-related to me, but they're sure as hell my brothers.

Suddenly, from the corner of my eye, I notice a flash of red through the growing dark.

It only lasted for an instant, but even just the crimson glint was enough to make my heart suddenly freeze in my chest.

What could that have been?

I twist my head to the side, searching for it in the field. No one else seems to have noticed it, but I can't look away. I feel drawn toward it, like it's magnetized me by some mythical force.

Then... I see her.

A woman with scarlet hair is walking away from the field. She's moving toward Coach's office, though I doubt the bloke would be in the mood to entertain any guests in the middle of his call. Frozen, I stare forward, mouth dropping as I take in the way her hips sway sensually with every step she takes. I wouldn't have even described the movement as walking. She was gliding. Every move she made caused my heart to throb.

She turns half to the side as though she could feel me looking and her face is illuminated in the dwindling light of the day. Green eyes sparkle like emeralds upon a sun-kissed face.

"You alright, bro?" Ryder asks, slight concern in his blue eyes as he stares at me in bewilderment. I can't imagine what my face must look like right now.

"Yeah, nah," I whisper before blinking hard and giving myself a rousing shake. "I mean yeah. I'm fine. I'm all good."

One of his dark eyebrows quirks upward. "I reckon maybe you've had too much sun, eh? It's gone to your head?"

I simply nod, glancing again across the field.

Something's gone to my head alright.

I swore off love. I swore off women... but judging by the erratic pulse of my heart and the lazy tendrils of desire that have begun to slither through my entire body, this girl might make me question everything.

## CHAPTER TWO

# Piper

Again, I bang on the office door before pressing my ear against it. I can hear someone inside, but they're either deaf or ignoring me. Seeing as none of my research into the Auckland rugby team has unveiled a deaf member, I'm inclined to believe the latter.

Irritation prickles at the back of my neck, lifting every hair on edge.

"Excuse me!" I call out. "My name is Piper! I'm with the Auckland paper. I just need a minute of your time for an interview-"

The door cracks open half an inch. The handsome, middle-aged man inside frowns at me starkly. "Sorry, miss. I have an important call right now. I can't be bothered with an interview."

"I'd only need just a few minutes!" I start to plead before the door is firmly shut in my face.

Groaning in frustration, I turn slowly around.

So much for that.

Sure, I reckon the professional thing to do might have been to make an appointment with the coach, but I needed a story – this story – bloody ASAP.

If I wanted to climb the ranks of the local paper where I'd been freshly employed, I needed to impress the editor. I'd thought handing in a face-to-face interview with someone affiliated with the Auckland team would fit the bill. Plus, it was no secret my editor loved rugby, which made the idea even sweeter.

Me? I didn't care much for rugby. In fact, I don't care much for athletes at all.

Not anymore, anyway.

I should have known I wouldn't be lucky enough to snag this interview. Nothing has gone right for me over the past few years. My life has left me feeling very much like a little ship battered by big waves.

With one last lingering glance over my shoulder at the office door, I begin to make my way back toward the parking lot.

I know I'm walking like a defeated woman. My shoulders are slouched, chin tucked, eyes down... but even still, I can feel someone's eyes on me.

At first, I keep my own gaze focused stubbornly ahead. I won't spare them a single glance. I muster up enough willpower to at least lift my chin, however.

After all, athletes are so not my type.

With their arrogance and sus behaviors and chiseled bodies and oh-so-sexy little shorts that perfectly show off their tanned, powerful legs – *No!*

"Now is not the time for that, Piper!" I scold myself sternly.

The last thing I need is yet another relationship that's doomed from the start. I've had enough of that. It's time to focus on me, only me. There's no bloody way I'm about to let a man drag me down again.

But, as I approach the parking lot, I feel the man's gaze slide down my body. I feel the burning heat of his laser-like vision mapping the curve of my hips and the way my hair trails down my spine... and I like it.

I more than like it. I want to feel desired. Attractive. Beautiful.

It's been so very long since I last felt that way.

I turn my head for just a second, sweeping the field before my emerald eyes lock on steel-grey orbs. In that single instant, an erotic bomb detonates deep in my body.

Heat surges through me, fireworks dancing across the backs of my eyelids as I give a dazed blink. This soul-shifting feeling is like nothing I've ever experienced before. His very existence hits me with the force of a fiery tsunami. Its wake crashes over me, burning through my veins until I'm quivering at the knees.

He stands slightly apart from the rest of the rugby players. He's not moving, simply content to stare.

Even from here, I can tell he's handsome. His blonde hair hangs into churning grey eyes.

I'd seen his picture before when I was researching the team. I know his name, Gray, but I had no idea he was going to incite this visceral reaction within my core.

I bite my lip hard, resisting the urge to lick my lips.

This is not good. Not good at all.

Suddenly breathless, I whip back around and dart toward my waiting car.

All I can do right now is escape and hope my body soon forgets this carnal craving.

## CHAPTER THREE

# Gray

Even against my closed eyelids, I can still see her; that mystery woman who might have me already wrapped around her pretty little finger.

I don't even know her name and she's all I can think about.

There was a part of me that wanted to chase her down after she left the field earlier, but I'd managed to hang onto some shred of restraint and prevent myself from acting like a total fool. Ryder would've never let me live it down if I'd gone sprinting after her. Hell, I reckon no one on the team would.

I keep telling myself that I don't need a woman in my life. I don't need any distraction.

After all, I know just how much damage a girl can do – and I'm not ready to brace my heart for any further pain.

Still... that doesn't prevent her face from rising in the back of my mind whenever I close my eyes.

She rises up in the distance, her tan skin glowing through the dark veil of my subconscious.

Her green eyes pierce the shadows, luring me closer. When I try to walk forward, I find I can't move. I'm stuck in place, bound by her beauty. I fight against the invisible shackles, desperate to stroke my fingertips over her body. To pull her into my chest. To cup her soft warmth in my rough palms until she cries out my name.

As I struggle to get closer to her yet still unable to move, she begins to vanish. Inch by beautiful inch, she's fading away into the dark.

I grunt and cry out, reaching toward her, and one single thought rings in my head.

*I should have never let her walk away.*

When our eyes locked, I could have sworn the air around me began to crackle. I wouldn't have been surprised if a thunderstorm blew through Auckland the very instant I spotted her. I'll never be able to forget the way her red hair clung to her coffee-colored cheeks, or the way her lips had just barely pursed while she was looking at me.

While the rest of the guys laughed and talked post-practice, my mind was only on her.

I know I can't let a woman distract me from the game, but that wasn't just any woman. Something intense sparked between us, something I don't understand.

It was like we were both supposed to be there. To see one another. Like we were both exactly where we were meant to be.

The last thing that remains of her in my dream are those haunting green eyes of hers. Just as they melt away, my body gives a jolt and my own eyes crack blearily open.

I sit up sharply, finding myself tangled in the sheets of my bed, my chest heaving as I stare around the room. I'm hunting for any trace of her even though I know that's impossible.

Every time I blink, I still see her in the recesses of my mind.

This is bloody insane. I reckon I'm going crazy.

I need to get out of my flat and get some fresh air or else I might end up just sitting in my room pining away for a woman I'll likely never see again.

I drag on my shoes and a pair of shorts, not even bothering to pull on a shirt before I rush out the door. It's a cool morning and lazy clouds float across the horizon as my feet thud against the sidewalk.

It's so early that most of Auckland is still asleep. A café has its doors propped open so that the scent of freshly baking muffins, bacon, and bitter coffee drift out into the street, beckoning in sleepy citizens of the city.

I just focus on moving forward, on placing one foot in front of the other so that I can leave that mysterious woman solidly in the past.

I'll never see her again, I remind myself. She and I will likely never cross paths in this busy city-

Suddenly, the tiniest dog I've ever seen shoots in front of me before skidding to a stop. Though it'd been running at a full sprint, it pauses now to look straight up at me. A leash hangs from around its collar.

"Uh, g'day, pup..." I say slowly, easing down so that I can snag the leash before he takes off again.

In the distance, I can hear a feminine voice shrieking, "Wait! Zeus, Wait!"

"I've got your boy, I think," I call back.

I shoot the tiny dog a skeptic glance. "Zeus, eh?" I say doubtfully, and he gives a little bark as if to tell me off.

The small creature stares intently at me, his black eyes and perked ears practically bigger than his head.

"Thank you so, so much!" the woman cries, falling to her knees beside me and reaching out to pet the dog. "He just slipped away from me."

"I really appreciate..." she trails off as I lift my head, her familiar green eyes going wide as saucers.

It's her. The woman from the field. The woman from my dreams. The woman I want more than anything.

### CHAPTER FOUR

# Piper

"Gray," I gasp out in shock, so startled to see the sexy rugby player that I can't even pretend not to know who he is.

He gazes at me with those gorgeous silver eyes of his, eyes I haven't stopped thinking about since dashing away from the rugby field yesterday.

I wonder if his parents knew he'd have those heart-melting silver eyes of his when they named him or if it was just a miraculous coincidence.

Does he remember me too?

There's likely no chance of that. A beloved athlete like him couldn't be bothered to etch the face of a smalltime journalist like me in his brain.

Besides, I know how athletes work. They think of themselves and their sport and nothing else.

Fumbling, I reach out for the dog's leash.

He playfully moves it just out of reach, a teasing smirk on his face. "You know my name. I reckon I deserve to know yours too, eh?"

The impish roguishness in his voice is enough to catch me a little off guard. Most athletes I know are too egocentric to have a sense of humor. It's yet another tempting layer to the sexy man.

"Piper," I stammer, hating the way my voice falters slightly.

Hopefully, he didn't notice it. If he had, he doesn't mention it.

"Piper," he echoes.

I swallow hard, the two syllables dancing against my eardrums. My lips part to beg him to say it again, but I swallow the plea and save at least some of my dignity.

"You were at the rugby field yesterday, right?" In one smooth movement, he passes me Zeus's leash.

When he pulls back, his fingertips just barely glide over my palm. My throat goes instantly tight, my tongue thick and heavy behind my teeth. I'm glad I'm kneeling down because if I'd been standing, I might have keeled right over.

Gulping, I nod. "I wanted to interview your coach but that didn't happen."

He laughs lightly. "Reckon so. He's pretty wound up at the moment."

My eyes skim over his shirtless, perfect body, every one of his muscles flawlessly toned from hours spent on the rugby field. It's no wonder Auckland has been doing so well this season with people like him on the field.

"Zeus?" he says, gesturing at my tiny dog.

Though Zeus is six years old, he's hardly bigger than a teacup. He's got more than enough personality to make up for his dwarfish size, however – and his bark is loud enough to scare away anybody from the door of my flat.

"He's small but fierce," I respond coolly, hoping that my voice doesn't tremble again.

As if on command, the pint-sized mutt gives a sharp growl, though his tail is wagging as he looks up at the rugby player.

"I see what you mean," Gray says with a loud, delighted laugh. He looks at Zeus with amusement shining in his grey eyes.

Slowly, the man extends a hand toward Zeus so the pup can sniff him.

"I wouldn't do that-" I start, but Zeus licks the man's hand.

What the hell?

My dog doesn't make friends. He makes victims. Any stray hand that isn't mine tends to get nipped. But this time Zeus, picky especially when it comes to men, actually seems willing to tolerate Gray. Maybe the athlete is a good guy, if those exist. Judging by my own history, it's not likely.

I toss my head slightly back and forth and then start to climb to my feet. It's just Zeus and I against the world these days. Zeus has been my one constant the past few years, and I'm not about to subject my dog to any more trials by fire like we'd been through lately. When you get involved with men, you're just asking for trouble.

"Anyway, thanks heaps for helping me out," I say hastily. I leap up to my feet, tugging at Zeus's leash. "We should really get going."

"Oi! You mean you're not even going to buy a bloke a coffee after he rescues your dog?" he calls after me.

I turn toward him, eyes widening just a hair as morning light dances across his body, highlighting every mouthwatering inch of him. He's grinning, and it's the most enticing, sincere smile I think I've ever seen in my life.

*Damn*, I whisper under my breath.

Before I can talk myself out of it, my chin ducks in a nod.

CHAPTER FIVE

# Gray

The walk to the nearby café is quiet and slightly awkward.

Zeus trots eagerly between us, his tail wagging enthusiastically. It seems his daring escape earlier wasn't enough excitement for the pooch. I steal glances at the stunning redhead beside me when I can, and when our gazes meet on occasion, my heart pounds in my chest.

I might be making a huge mistake in inviting her out for coffee, but after I regretted her slipping away earlier so much, I just couldn't help myself. I know women can't be trusted, but this one has already gotten under my skin. I just hope this spontaneous little date doesn't end with me regretting it all.

We settle down at an outside table of the café with two cups of coffee and Zeus patiently laying beneath my seat. Every so often, as if to remind me that he's there, he gives my sneaker a little nip to remind me to be nice to his best friend.

Piper seems stunned by how the pup has taken to me, and though I'd considered myself a cat person up until this point, even I have to admit the dog is endearing. Something about his cartoonish, larger than life features on his itty-bitty little body is bloody adorable.

Plus, how can you not love a dog named Zeus?

"So..." she says, dipping her spoon in her mug and giving it a little swirl.

When she looks at me, I can't tell if she's blushing or if she's just warming up with the morning sunlight. Either way, she's beautiful. I don't want to blink and miss even a second of her.

"So, you said you wanted to interview Coach, right?" I ask.

She nods, brightening slightly.

"Yes, I work for the local paper. I just started recently so I'm trying to build a name for myself. I was hoping for an interview with someone on your team would give me a nice boost, especially with how well you lot are performing in the National Cup matches."

Though Piper had been acting a little shy, that seems to melt away as she starts talking about her job. But, just as quickly as she became more buoyant and happy, she deflates again.

"But I reckon I've lost my chance," she sighs. "My deadline is in two days and I don't think your coach will have a spare second."

I stroke my chin, a faint smirk dancing on my face. "Then how about you interview me, eh? You just need someone on the team, right?"

She chokes on the drink and those green eyes of hers get big again.

"Really?" she gasps.

When I nod, she gives an elated, sweet cry of happiness.

She leans eagerly forward toward me, gently grabbing my hand. Her fingers are warm and soft as she grips me. Zeus's collar rattles as he perks up, watching us intently to make sure there's no funny business happening. Heat surges up my arm from where it forms under her hand, the flames licking at my heart and making every one of my muscles clench with desire.

I'd give bloody anything to have her run those hands over my body.

"You're a lifesaver!" she continues before releasing me.

Even after she stops touching me, the heat refuses to fade. It just continues to build. Lust simmers in my core, leaving my entire body feeling like its vibrating from the intensity of my longing for Piper's touch.

Piper digs through her bag, dragging out a pencil and a notepad.

Chuckling, I grin at her. "Just make sure say in the article that I'm not just a superstar, smokin' hot rugby player, but that I rescue helpless animals in my spare time."

She smiles right back at me, rolling her eyes playfully. "I'll see what I can do... But let's get started. How long have you been on the team? Any words of wisdom you'd say for young hopefuls who want to be in your striped jersey one day? What about comments for your opponents?"

"Almost two years. Never give up. And prepare for a hiding,' I respond, ticking her questions off one by one.

She nods as I talk, her pencil flicking across her paper with lightning speed.

"And what do you think about your chances of winning the National Cup? What'll be the first thing you do if you get that trophy?"

Her questions rapidly spill out of her mouth, her face bright and energetic. I've never seen anyone as passionate about anything, aside from perhaps when Jax is flying across the rugby field. They have the same expression: pure devotion to the craft. It's admirable, and in the case of the gorgeous redhaired woman in front of me, adorable.

As she's scribbling frantically away while I answer her questions, I notice a thin pale band of skin around her left-hand ring finger. Slowly, my heart begins to sink. At one point, a ring was there. A wedding band, no doubt.

Was Piper married?

When she notices me staring, she clears her throat and places her hand in her lap. Suddenly, her questions have stopped.

"How about I interrogate you now?" I quip, eager to get more details about the beautiful scarlet-haired bombshell seated across from me.

There's no trace of her vibrant smile any longer. She frowns, lips pursing.

"Actually, I think I better go," she says hurriedly, pushing back from the table. She hadn't even finished her coffee. Something I said must have rubbed her the wrong way.

Guilt seeps through me, as does confusion.

Just who is Piper?

"Thanks again for catching Zeus and for letting me interview you," she says, digging through her bag for a few dollars.

I reach over, pushing her cash back toward her.

She pauses, head cocking just slightly as her redhaired brow crinkles.

"Don't you know?" I murmur with a teasing smirk, "A gentleman pays on the first date."

"I..." Piper stammers, more flustered than she was even when she bumped into me this morning. She takes one stumbling step back and then another. She won't meet my eyes. "Zeus, come on, boy!"

Before I can even react, she's yet again running away.

Piper is truly a woman of mystery. She's a puzzle that I want to put slowly together, agonizing over each and every piece. She's a riddle I'm dying to solve.

But how am I going to do that now that she's gone again?

It's then that I notice something resting in her chair. I reach over, picking it up, and realize it's her wallet. A slow smile spreads across my face.

Maybe this chapter isn't closed after all.

CHAPTER SIX

# Piper

The door to my flat slams behind me as I sprint inside like hell itself is on my heels.

Zeus barks a few times, looking at the door as though he's asking why we had to leave Gray so abruptly.

I don't answer him, choosing instead to head into the kitchen. I move like I'm on some frenzied form of autopilot. My legs erratically stomp, my arms wildly swing, my heart feverishly pounds. I can hardly see, there are so many spots swirling in front of my vision.

As quickly as I can, I grab a glass and fill it with cool water before gulping every last drop down. The ice-cold drink does nothing to dim the flames soaring up from the depths of my body. Heat pulses between my thighs so intensely that I have to press my knees roughly together. My whole body tingles, even just the way my shirt lightly shifts against my breasts making fireworks erupt in my stomach.

I have no idea what Gray has done to me.

Sitting across from him outside that café, I had to do my best to pay attention to what he was saying, because I was so enraptured with the way his handsome mouth formed every single word. I could sit and listen to him talk about nothing for hours, if he'd let me.

But, at the same time, my heart gives a violent throb.

How could I have only just met this man, and already I'm falling head over heels from him.

Anxiously, I brush my fingers over my left hand, trying to remind myself what happened last time I allowed myself to fall for someone. I'd thought I'd cared about that person, that he'd cared about me, and yet he walked away and broke my heart.

Then again, I'd never felt even a fraction of the burning fire I feel for Gray for anyone else.

What does it mean?

What am I supposed to believe?

Sensing my distress, Zeus puts a concerned paw on my leg and I bend down to stroke his ears.

I close my eyes, begging the throbbing pulse within my body to ebb. At this rate, I'm going to need a bloody cold shower just to start thinking straight.

I'd gotten my story, I know shouldn't want anything to do with Gray... and yet, all I want is to see him again.

Suddenly, there's a knock at the door. It's a short but powerful knock, and at the sound, Zeus whines and rushes toward it. He sniffs the air and then begins to excitedly bark, his tail wagging frantically.

I'd never seen my dog act like this before... and there's only one other person he seems to like besides me.

Biting my lip, I walk forward. I stand there, just beyond the wood, staring at the closed door. I could pretend I'm not home. I could ignore him.

Then, life would go back to normal...

Or I could be bold. I could be brave.

Even just for one bloody second, I could put my heart on the line again.

Against my better judgment, I pull open the door.

Gray's strong, still shirtless figure fills the doorway. Without speaking, he lifts his hand. In his palm, my wallet rests.

Had I really forgotten it? Can I convince myself that was just an accident? Or was I leaving some sort of calling card for the handsome man.

"You left something behind," he muses, holding it out to me.

I reach out and take the wallet, sparks sizzling down my arm when my fingers brush his. I move to pull away, but he gently grips my wrist.

"I never got the chance to say goodbye, Piper," he murmurs. His tone is deep and gruff.

I have to bite back a moan when he says my name.

"What if I left as quickly as I did so that I wouldn't have to hear you say it?" I whisper back.

I don't even recognize my own voice. It's rich and throaty and full of longing.

He wets his lips, releasing my wrist so that he can gently grip my hips. I melt forward toward him, chin tipping up before his arm slips around my waist.

For a long, throbbing moment, we just gaze into one another's eyes.

Can he feel my heart battering my ribs? Can he sense how much I want him?

"You're so bloody beautiful, Piper..." he says, fingertips digging lightly into my back.

Breathlessly, I plead, "Then kiss me."

With a primal growl, Grays' mouth descends roughly upon mine and I lose myself in the crimson wave of passion burning through me.

CHAPTER SEVEN

# Gray

Piper moans against my lips as I lift her up in my arms, pressing her back against the wall of her apartment. Her legs twine around my waist. The tip of her velvet tongue brushes my lower lip and I grunt with eager desire.

With her in my arms, everything feels right.

"My bedroom," she pants, breaking the kiss only long enough to suck in a shallow breath of air and gesture toward a nearby door.

I carry her into the room and we collapse together against soft lavender sheets. Her sweet, subtle fragrance fills the room. It wafts from the pillows and the blankets and her clothes. It's intoxicating and I can't get enough.

Trying to remember not to be too greedy or rough, I free Piper from her clothes while tearing at my own. All I want is to be intertwined with the redheaded beauty gazing at me with alluring green eyes. When our naked flesh presses together, she moans again.

I grip her wrists easily in one of my strong hands, pinning her arms over her head as my other hand explores her. I turn her face so I can kiss her delicious mouth before nipping at her jaw and suckling at her neck. Her back arches as a light bruise forms under my lips on the delicate flesh of her neck.

"Gray...!" she cries out, legs twining around me, drawing me toward her.

She pants as my lips descend the curve of her breast. Her hips grind against mine, tormenting me.

I return to her lips, kissing her roughly. I can't be gentle anymore. Judging by the lustful smile on her face, she wouldn't have it any other way.

My whole body throbs with need as I gaze into her eyes, my swollen, aching shaft slowly beginning to thrust inside of her. Her slick, smooth inner muscles clench around me, begging for more.

A roar of ecstasy ripples up my throat as I bury myself completely inside her in one strong stroke, causing her eyes to roll back and her legs to tighten even more around me so she can relish every single rock-hard inch.

Clinging to one another, we rock together. My mouth ravishes hers as our tongues wrestle with primal passion. I can no longer tell where she begins and I end. All I know is that I want this moment to last forever.

But she feels so bloody good that pure, raw ecstasy is already welling within me. Every stroke brings me closer to the edge. I release her hands and she runs them through my hair, knotting at the base of my scalp. She bucks against me, yearning for more. My fingers explore the dips and curves of her smooth skin.

Her voice begins to pitch higher, all but screaming my name as her body clenches against me. Wave after wave of pleasure rolls through her as she trembles in my arms. The look of sheer pleasure in her dazed eyes and the way she whimpers with bliss is too much for me to bear. My own passion overwhelms me. As stars burst in front of my eyes, I pin her down and bury myself deep inside her one more time.

We lay there, panting, holding one another close as daylight continues to filter in through her window.

I know practice is going to start soon, but I can't imagine being anywhere but here.

My fingers lace with hers and I lift her left hand gently to my lips. She smiles at first, but then her eyes shift toward the ring finger of that hand and it quickly fades. She bites her lip and tries to hide it from me.

"You were married?" I ask softly.

She hesitates, almost pulling away, but I embrace her tighter. The last thing I want is any distance between us.

"I got divorced last year, but the marriage was over way before then. We'd dated since we were in high school. I felt like marriage was just the next step, you know?"

I nod quietly, continuing to watch her.

"After the divorce, I started thinking about what I want from my life. That's when I started working for the paper. It was something all of my own, something that I believed in, that I was proud of.

It'd always been my dream, but he'd always told me that I wasn't cut out for journalism."

A possessive fire flares within me.

How could anyone look in Piper's eager green eyes and tell her she wasn't cut out for anything? Hadn't he seen what I did when she was interviewing me? Hadn't he seen how passionate she was?

Good bloody riddance.

I stroke her face, brushing her hair back.

"What about you?" she murmurs. "How's a sexy, suave rugby star like you still single?"

"I got cheated on," I answer frankly.

Her eyes widen slightly as her cheeks flame red. "I'm sorry, I shouldn't have said anything. I can never keep my bloody mouth shut when it matters."

I just shrug. "It's all good. It's been a while now."

My cool tone hides the mulling thoughts whirling in my head. After finding my girlfriend in bed with another man, I'd sworn off romance... yet here I was, snuggling a woman in her bed while my rugby teammates were out on the field.

I want to be here with Piper. I want to pretend the world doesn't exist outside this room. I want to act like neither one of us has ever been hurt in the name of love... but I also have some thinking to do.

Am I ready for this – whatever *this* is? Is she ready?

I suddenly can't imagine my life without Piper in it, but what does that mean?

Sensing the shift in my mood, Piper pulls away. This time, as much as it kills me, I let her go.

"...I should get to work on my piece," she says softly.

I nod and slowly climb off the bed. "I should get to practice anyway."

I start to dress, pulling on my shorts and finding my socks. The whole time, she sits on the bed and gazes at me. When I've finished getting my clothes on, I look back at her one last time. She's wrapped in the sheet, her red hair mussed, her beautiful face serious, the sun illuminating her like a beacon.

I can't resist returning to her, grabbing her face and kissing her one more time. She kisses me back with equal passion, as though she's afraid this might be the last kiss we ever have.

Would today be both the beginning and ending of something remarkable? Am I leaving out of fear?

My head pulses with confusion. I just don't know what the right choice is.

However, even as I'm leaving her flat, I can't shake the feeling that leaving her bed is the worst mistake I've ever made.

## CHAPTER EIGHT

# Piper

It's been three long days since I last heard from Gray.

I'd kept my cool, but every minute that passes without him calling me is driving me crazy. He's the first man I've been with since my divorce, and the moment had been so intimate and passionate and amazing on every level. I'm left craving not only Gray's touch, but also the way he'd looked at me, and the way he'd said my name, and the way I fit in his arms.

Does he Gray feel like that? Does he not long for me too?

Am I just being foolish?

Then, from my pocket, my phone suddenly vibrates.

I suppress a cry of eager surprise and wrench it free... but it's just a text from my editor. Since handing over my interview, I hadn't heard anything back from her. With my luck lately, I reckon she thought it was pure garbage and just discarded it.

To my surprise, however, the text is a cheerful one.

*Loved the piece*! My editor has written. *I've gotten it published. Here's the link. We should have a chat about your future here on Monday. I've got big things in mind for you!*

Eyes widening, I tap the URL that my editor included in the text. Immediately, I'm brought to a page of the paper's website. I give a gasp, scrolling through the page. My interview had only been up a short while, but the comments were already flooding in – and there was my name, right at the top. A swell of pride ripples through me.

I'd done it. I'd really done it.

As I'm skimming the text, a picture of Gray fills the screen. I bite my lip, gazing down at his handsome face.

You know what? Screw this. Screw bloody all of this.

I'm tired of waiting around to hear from him. I'm tired of waffling between disappointment and longing.

I deserve to know where Gray stands. I've wasted too much of my time on a guy with no real interest in me before.

Jamming my phone in my pocket, I hightail it to the field where I know the Auckland team will be practicing.

It's a good thing I didn't hesitate either. By the time I arrive, it seems the practice is over and the boys are beginning to leave. I skim the field, frowning as I search for his familiar figure amongst the rest.

I find him standing next to a dark-haired player... and two female fans who've just rushed onto the field.

Even from over here, I can hear him and the other man laughing. They hug the girls, idly chatting... and suddenly, I feel like a fool. Of course he's going to have girls all over him. That one day with me was nothing but a fling to him.

After all, that's how athletes are. My husband was an athlete too, and I'd always said I'd never get wrapped up in another one.

I whip around so my back is to Gray, pressing my palms against my eyes as tears begin to well.

What am I doing here? Why am I chasing this man? Why was I willing to put myself out on that narrow limb, knowing it would snap beneath me and send me crashing down into heartache?

I'm the one to blame for feeling like this.

I need to go. I need to put as much space between Gray and myself as possible.

But just as I take one lurching step forward, a hand coils around my wrist and lightly spins me around.

CHAPTER NINE

# Gray

"Piper! You're here," I murmur happily.

I start to pull her against me, but the redhaired woman jerks slightly away. A lone tear streaks down her tan cheek.

That same defensive possessiveness that I feel whenever I'm around the green-eyed journalist again begins to blaze. "What's wrong? Did someone hurt you? Are you alright?"

"I'm bloody fine," she hisses in a voice that tells me she is certainly not bloody fine.

Gently, I grip her shoulders, gazing into her eyes. Pain eddies there, and I'm positive that I caused it.

"Tell me what I did," I urge her.

I can feel a few of the guys watching us, but I can't be bothered to pay any attention to them right now. All that matters is Piper. These last three days, all I've done is miss her. All I've done is crave being with her again.

The more time that passed, the more certain I was that I need her in so many ways. I need not only her kiss but her spunk and her zeal. I want her, all of her.

She bites her lip hard and blinks furiously, trying to contain her tears. "Where have you been, Gray? Why haven't I heard from you?"

I sigh and shake my head, releasing her shoulders only so I can grasp her hands. I lift them and press them against my heart. She clings to my shirt, looking up at me with an expression of frustration and uncertainty.

I hate that I'm the root of that.

"I just wanted us to have some space to think, Piper. You said you'd felt like you were just making the motions with your ex-husband. That you got married just because you thought you had to. I didn't want you to think that just because you and I slept together that you had to give me your heart."

Her teeth grit slightly. "You don't think I'm mature enough to know my own feelings, Gray? You don't trust that I'm capable of making that decision myself?"

I gaze at her, considering her words. She stares right back, chin lifted and eyes narrowed. I have so much admiration for her in this moment. I'd hurt her, albeit accidentally, and she has the strength to tell me exactly what's on her mind. That makes her even more wonderous to me. She truly is special and magnificent in every way.

"You're right," I answer simply.

"...I am?" she says, caught off guard that I would admit it so readily.

I step closer, closing the distance between us. She tips her head up to look at me, eyes momentarily flitting across my mouth. Her pupils dilate slightly as she breathes in the scent of salt and grass and sweat on my body.

"I shouldn't have vanished like that. I should have spoken to you, Piper. The moment I left, I knew I was making a mistake... and that terrified me. It terrified me how much I already cared about you. It terrified me that I would already do anything for you. I'd devote my life to bloody lassoing the moon if you asked. I've never felt this way about anyone. On some level, I didn't reach out to you because I was terrified that you wouldn't want me like I wanted you – but that was selfish."

"If it terrified you then, how does it make you feel now?" she whispers.

I part my lips to speak, but no words quite suited the maelstrom of emotions surging through me.

So, instead, I release her hands and cup her face. She softly moans my name the moment my fingers brush her cheeks, allowing me to pull her closer so that my lips can taste hers again.

She leans into me, her arms looping around my neck. Behind us, the guys on the team start to hoot and holler.

We break away to breathe, though stay locked in one another's arms, and she blinks as if clearing stars from her eyes.

"It makes me feel like I love you, Piper," I whisper, just in case she couldn't gather that from the deep, passionate kiss. "I never want to be away from you. I want your face to be the first one I see in the morning and the last I see at night. I want to walk Zeus with you. I want to curl up with you on the couch. I want to hear you cheering for me when we win the National Cup." I pause and then repeat, "I love you," with as much sincerity as I can muster. "I will never hurt you again."

The tears in her eyes pour down her cheeks as she clings to my wrists, her eyes getting bigger and bigger with every word that comes from my lips.

"I love you too!" she gushes finally. "Oh, Gray... everything just makes sense when I'm with you. I feel more myself than I ever have before. I just feel... complete with you. Total. Whole."

Laughing, I lift her up and spin her before setting her back down. As we exchange kiss after kiss, my rugby brothers continue to cheer.

I have no doubt that Piper and I were meant to meet and I have no doubt that my soulmate is safe in my arms now, just as I have no doubt that she and I are two perfect puzzle pieces finally clicking into place.

## EPILOGUE

# Piper

"Where are we going?" I giggle, clinging to Gray's hand as he guides me forward.

Before leaving our flat, Gray had requested to blindfold me for some surprise he had planned. I had no idea where we were.

"We're almost there," he whispers in his ear, his hot breath drifting across my neck.

Suddenly, he pulls the blindfold away. For a moment, I have to blink hard so that I can clear my vision and look around. Then I gasp, hands flying to my face in shock. We're at the rugby field where Gray practices, however the place has been decorated with flowers and candles and a picnic blanket is spread across the grass. Zeus patiently waits for us there, giving a bark of greeting and wagging his tail.

"Gray! What is this?" I gasp.

He takes my hands in his and smiles softly. "This is the place where you and I first locked eyes," he says. "This is the place where I found the love of my life."

I bite my lip, my heart throbbing in my chest from his sweet words. I can't help but lean closer and kiss him gently. He wraps me up in his arms and I close my eyes, cherishing the moment. Being with him continues to be perfect in every way. Every day, I wake up feeling like the luckiest girl in the entire world.

"It's been a whole year, Piper," he says with a big smile. "A whole year of laughing and loving. A whole year of bliss. I wanted to celebrate that in a special way."

I laugh and tug away to scamper over toward the picnic blanket. All of my favorite things have been set out. There are little cakes and a bottle of wine and a charcuterie spread.

Somehow, Zeus had resisted the urge to help himself thus far.

"When did you find time to put all this together?" I ask giddily.

Gray chuckles and follows after me. "I had a little help from my brothers on the team."

"This is so sweet, Gray. Thank you!" I lean down to open the bottle of wine, and as I do, something sparkles on Zeus's collar.

"What've you go there, boy?" I ask, reaching forward to check it out. Before I can touch him, he trots toward Gray.

When I turn around, Gray is kneeling before me, holding Zeus in his arms.

"...What are you doing?" I ask, suddenly breathless. My heart pulses faster and faster as excitement makes my palms go clammy.

Gray just grins, fiddling with Zeus's collar for a moment before setting him down. The tiny pooch sits patiently at Gray's side, looking between us with a doggy smile.

"Piper, I love you so much," Gray begins, "...I want to spend my life with you."

He lifts up the sparkly object he'd pulled from Zeus's collar, revealing the most beautiful diamond ring I've ever seen.

"Will you marry me?" he asks, his voice husky and deep.

"Yes!" I cry out, allowing him to slide the ring on my hand. "Oh, Gray! I would love to be your wife!"

Gray laughs, scooping up Zeus and standing so that he can hug both of us. Zeus licks both of our cheeks.

The first time I'd been proposed to, I knew it wasn't right. I knew it wouldn't make me happy. But this time, there isn't a shadow of a doubt that I'm making the right choice.

Gray dips me back, kissing me tenderly, and I hug him tight.

This time last year, I'd felt so alone and lost, but now I know that everything I went through was meant to guide me into Gray's arms.

It was a chance of fate that brought Gray and I into one another's lives, but it's true love that will keep us together forever.

The End

# RYDER

CHAPTER ONE

# Ryder

Music from the nightclub across the street pulses through the cool night air. The beat throbs, punctuated by the occasional sound of girls giggling and blokes working their best pickup lines.

I don't know why those guys are even trying. They ain't got nothing on my suave skill. I'll have all the ladies drooling over me the second I make my grand entrance. It's one of the perks of being the sexiest man on the Auckland rugby team. That's not just overconfidence either. It's the bloody truth... as far as I'm concerned anyway.

"Come on, bro!" I groan loudly, shifting my cell from one ear to the other. "Why are you being so lame, Jax? It's not like you've got a girl to keep you home. Come party with me for once!"

Jax, another player on the Auckland Rugby Union team, just chuckles.

"Sorry, man. I'm exhausted. And with the National Cup just around the corner, I can't be bothered-"

"The Cup is two months away!" I protest, glancing over my shoulder at the raging club behind me.

The New Zealand city is ready to party the night away, but none of my teammates seem keen to join in. I'd already invited Gray and Manu out, only to have them bail at the last second. I'd tried my best mate too, though he was the only bloke with a halfway decent excuse. Kai was meeting up with his parents, a rare occasion seeing as they practically disowned him for pursuing a career in rugby.

Some people just don't get the comradery that comes with a team like ours. We're more than just a bunch of blokes barreling across a field at the same time. We're family, and family is what counts the most; it counts more than anything. That's a lesson you have to learn the hard way.

My heart gives a painful throb and I clench my teeth before refocusing on the club. I'd come out tonight to forget my emotions, not to get wrapped up in them.

"Sorry, bro," Jax continues. "I want to get up early to practice. We're going up against the team from Manu's hometown in a few weeks, and God knows each of them is as big and burly as he is."

Jax does have a point about that. Manu is beefy as hell and I reckon the Taranaki team is full of his not-so-mini-mes. However, that doesn't change the fact that I'm intending to lose myself in the arms of some beautiful, random woman tonight. When my sheets are cold, my heart feels even colder. I need someone to warm me up and keep that hollow iciness at bay.

"More girls for me then, I guess," I sigh, hanging up on Jax and rolling my eyes.

Plunging the phone into my pocket, I march inside. The bouncer gives me a nod, letting me pass by the growing line of partygoers desperate to get into the exclusive hotspot. I practically have an all-access pass.

Lights flash as bodies bump and grind together on the dance floor. I skim the room, wondering which gorgeous woman will help while away my evening. I hate being alone, even for a second.

"You're Ryder, right?" gasps a pretty young thing by the bar. She clasps her hands together, her wide eyes rounding. "You're on the Auckland team! You guys are on a roll this season, eh?"

"That's right, babe," I answer with a wink. "How ya going?"

"Amazing now," she giggles, eyelashes fluttering.

I've got her. Hook, line, sinker.

It's easy enough. As soon as the ladies realize who I am and what team I play for, they're putty in my hands. There's no work, no effort. I like it that way, or at least, that's what I tell myself. I've never had to work for anything. I was born with money and good looks. I made it onto the Auckland team the first time I tried out. Now it looks like we're going to breeze all the way to the National Cup trophy. Life is simple. Isn't that best?

"You're in luck tonight," I continue smoothly. "We didn't have practice today so I reckon my muscles are in peak condition for a little spin on the dancefloor."

"Really?" she exclaims giddily. She pauses for a moment, eyes briefly skimming the crowded club. "By the way, Manu or Kai didn't happen to come with you tonight, did they...?"

"What?" I gasp, dignity wounded. "Why would anyone care whether Manu or Kai came out tonight? I'm the life of the party!"

"Because everyone knows they're the two best looking and best playing Auckland blokes," a feminine voice retorts from across the bar.

"Now hold on a bloody second," I scoff, whirling toward the woman.

Her golden eyes boldly blaze into my blue ones and the force of them is enough to knock my whole world off its axis.

"Hello again, Ryder. Been a while, eh?" she muses, beautiful head cocking to the side.

I take in her familiar beauty, stunned by the fact that my childhood rival is even more lovely than she was back in our school days.

The cute girl I'd been chatting up a second ago has already faded from my mind, but Stella... now she is a woman you never forget.

Believe me when I say she wouldn't let you.

## CHAPTER TWO

# Stella

"You've really made a name for yourself, haven't you?" I grin.

Ryder's face, momentarily blank with surprise, melts back into his typical smug smirk... an expression that, even after all these years, makes my heart flutter.

He's always had that effect on me, even when we were butting heads as kids in school.

"You bet your sweet ass I have," he responds, voice a purr. "And that is one sweet ass you've got, Stells."

A rogue shudder rolls through me.

"It's Stella, Ryder," I correct.

His lips twitch further apart. "To me, you'll always be Stells."

As infuriating as Ryder has always been, he's also always been too damn sexy for his own good. It's no wonder all the women in town trip all over themselves just to be even the briefest focus of those beautiful blues of his.

Tall and lean yet buff, the dark-haired rugby player gives a wolfish whistle as his eyes rake over my body. He takes his time looking me up and down, the greedy glint of his eyes enough to make heat coil in my core. My veins simmer and I take another drink of my wine to douse it, though it only seems to spur the flames licking up inside of me to burn brighter.

He sidles closer, completely ignoring the woman he'd been hitting on a moment ago. If I were a less self-respecting woman, I'd have been proud of the fact that I was enough to distract him from a sensual target. Oh, hell, I am proud of it.

"So, what are you doing in a place like this?" he quips. "Still stalking me?"

My eyes roll so far back I can practically see into my skull.

"Me, stalking you? Please. We both know it was the other way around. Every time I turned around, there you were. You were always just a step behind, eh? I was always top of the class, head of our clubs, fastest on the track."

Ryder's eyes churn as he slides an arm against the countertop. His fingers barely brush across the flesh of my arm, but the skin erupts with tingles. I resist the urge to gasp, though I feel my nostrils flare.

He leans a little closer. "What can I say? Being behind you was always a little more fun. Didn't I mention your sweet ass already, Stells?"

My knees are beginning to quiver.

As much as I don't like to admit it, there's always been a certain amount of tension between Ryder and myself. I've always wanted him, and I reckon he's always wanted me, but I also am completely aware of the way he operates. Ryder is a please them and leave them type of guy. One night only. Plus, that cocky attitude is almost too much to handle.

But, then again... I have been working so hard lately... would it be so wrong to have a few hours of fun?

I bite down on my lip hard. Should I even be entertaining this idea? Ryder is so not my type. I like the serious guys. You know the type. Business suits, slicked-back hair, the ones that are easy to walk all over. Ryder, he's more like an untamable stallion, but I sure could use a wild ride right about now.

"What are you doing here?" he asks, gesturing around. "I reckon this isn't your typical haunt, eh?"

"Networking. The environmental nonprofit I work for needs donations and the blokes who come here are typically rolling in cash." I toss my hair over my shoulder, daring him to degrade my choice of profession.

Back in the day, I used to talk a big game about becoming a lawyer some day or something equally prestigious that would net me billions. Instead, I was drawn toward the small firm I call my vocational home these days. We don't make any money, but we make New Zealand a better place one legislative action at a time.

To my surprise, his brows lift with faint interest. It's perhaps the first time I've seen him intrigued by anything not directly involving him. Maybe even Ryder has grown up a bit.

"Straight up? And here I thought you'd be dominating the world by now."

"I am," I answer, giving him a taste of his own haughty attitude. This seems to attract him even more, as his smile widens. I always was the only one willing to dish out what he served up. "I'm just doing it on my own terms. And you? What are you doing here? Looking for a lucky lady to lead on for a few hours?"

His tongue drags against his upper lip as he appraises me. There's a blatant hunger in his eyes as he looks at me that's unlike any other way I've ever been looked at before. The smirk on my face fades slightly, my heart picking up its pace.

"That's exactly what I'm doing," he murmurs huskily. He leans closer, breath hot against my ear. "How about you, Stells? Will you be my lucky lady tonight?"

The hand near my arm gently grasps my elbow, fingertips digging into the prickling flesh. The hair on the back of my neck lifts like it's been electrified by his touch. The heat in my core flares, causing my thighs to clench as my whole body throbs with desire.

I could say no. Hell, I should say no.

I know all about Ryder and what he wants... but just this once, I want to let loose. I want to be wild. I want a taste of something I can never have.

"I don't know about lucky," I whisper, turning my face to his, "but I'll be yours for one night only."

## CHAPTER THREE

# Ryder

I can hardly believe my luck.

Here I am, walking out of the club with Stella on my arm.

I never expected her to give me a shot, but I suppose even someone as straitlaced as Stella needs some fun every now and then – and I intend to make this night very, very fun.

Stells and I have always had a hot and cold relationship. She could be a total ice queen, but, at the same time, this rivalry of ours runs blisteringly hot. She's sexy, sassy, and so beautiful it almost hurts to look at her. She's the total package, and for just a little while, she'll be all mine.

"I live just around the corner," she says, nodding her head down the street.

I nod, grateful that Stella lives close seeing as my little sister is back at my own flat. As much of a dog as I reckon I am, I don't like brazenly bringing home ladies when Jade is there. She's been through enough; she doesn't need to deal with my dalliances too. I sneak them in and I sneak them out, trying to keep my sister none the wiser.

The breeze is chilly as it wraps around us, but it does nothing to smother the burning desire I have for Stella. I've pined after her as long as I can remember, but she's never so much as entertained the idea of us hooking up. Until now, at least.

The walk to the apartment is quick and quiet, but neither one of us can seem to stop touching the other. My hand roams across her back, feeling the heat of her flesh from beneath the thin fabric of her black dress. She's looped one arm around my waist, her fingers delicately plunged just beneath my belt. The glances we exchange are heated and desperate.

The moment her key is thrust into the lock and the door swings open, we're upon one another. Even just that brief walk from the club was far too long. The tension that's always been between us has reached its breaking point.

I scoop her into my arms the second we cross the threshold, hungry lips finding hers. She moans softly as she leans into the kiss, but I want to make her scream.

I head into the bedroom, lightly tossing her onto the bed. Before she's even landed on her soft sheets, I'm on top of her. My mouth blazes a trail across her jaw so that I can nip at her ear. Her back arches, breathing already heavy, her eyes rolling back as her legs twine around my hips. Her eyes crack open as she grins at me, her thighs tightening as she rolls us across the sheets.

She straddles me, giggling faintly as she grabs her dress in her hands and pulls it up and over her head.

"You naughty minx," I laugh, though the sound is throaty and deep. "Nothing beneath that dress, eh? I'm starting to believe you had some wicked intentions tonight."

Stella just grins impishly at me. She grabs my shirt, ripping it off my muscled body.

The moon shimmers in through her window, dancing along the supple curves of her body. She's so damn gorgeous that for a moment I go completely still so I can worship her with my eyes. Her cheeks flame slightly pink as she leans down to kiss me again.

The instant she moves, I grip her hips, rolling us back over so that she's beneath me again. She gasps, eyes rounding as the smile on her face widens. She paws at my pants until I've shimmied out of them and kicked them across the room.

My body collapses back against hers, feeling the heat of her entire body pressing against my own. I inhale, her fragrance sweet and familiar and intoxicating.

Every inch of me is begging to ravish her, and yet, for some reason, I take my time.

I grab her hands, moving to pin them over her head. The moment I press her wrists against her pillows, our fingers instinctively lace. Her eyes pour into mine as our noses brush, my lips capturing hers again.

Our eyes remain locked, the kiss so intense it threatens to blow my mind. I press her hard against the bed, suddenly desperate not just to sleep with her, but to be one with her. It's a visceral urge that I don't understand – that I've never felt before.

All I really know is that I can't deny it.

I've never felt this turned on before. My body is practically screaming for Stella, and I can feel the throbbing heat of her own powerful desire against the shaft of my pulsing manhood.

I can't resist a moment longer.

In one powerful stroke, I bury myself within Stella. Her head tips back, her mouth breaking from mine as she gives a feral, sharp shriek of pure pleasure. She clings to me, fingernails digging into the backs of my hands as she begs for more.

Again and again, we rock together, kissing and staring into one another's eyes and clinging to one another. Our clenched fingers never unlace.

Even as pleasure swells inside of me, my pace never slows. I can't get enough of her velvet warmth or her soft kiss. Beneath me, her entire body begins to spasm. She screams my name so loud that I'm sure her whole building hears it. I smother her with kisses, muffling the noise even as my own ecstasy peaks.

Our chests heave as we fall against her sheets. I release her hands only so that her arms can twine around me, and I pull her against my chest so that I can kiss her face.

I've never felt the urge to stay with any one woman I've slept with... but there's something about Stella that's hooked me instead of the other way around. I don't want to go. I want to hold her all night long. I'm not quite sure what to do with those feelings.

She lifts her chin and rests it on my chiseled pec, smiling breathlessly at me.

Just the sight of her makes fireworks dance across my vision. It isn't just the intense sex that's left me reeling... it's her.

"Stella..." I start to whisper, but I'm interrupted by the trill of my cell across my room.

My entire heart clenches as she withdraws from me, dragging her hands through her mussed hair.

"You should answer that," she murmurs, her back turning toward me.

I reach out, wanting to run my fingers down her spine, but then the phone rings again. Reluctantly, I climb out of the bed to get it.

CHAPTER FOUR

# Stella

Laying here in my bed that now smells headily of Ryder, I've never been more confused in my life.

I inhale slightly, tasting his cologne and the fragrance of his body mixed with my own familiar perfume. The scent is enough to make my mouth water for more of the blue-eyed rugby player.

He and I had always clashed, but now I'm overwhelmed by the desire to curl up against him again. Growing up, he'd always been so bold and brash and I know how he goes through women with the same chaotic fervency he must go through socks, but the way he'd looked in my eyes while we were twined together and the way he'd touched me and the way he'd kissed me... it all felt so strangely passionate and real and intimate.

But how?

How could I be feeling those things for Ryder?

Had he felt them too?

Sitting up slowly, I gather my sheets around me. My body is vibrating with ecstasy and every so often another ripple of pleasure shudders through me. I lift my hands, looking at them, thinking about what it felt like to cling to Ryder's strong and rough palms. I don't do one-night stands. I do relationships. But that single romp had more passion to it than any of my past escapades had.

Ryder, still naked, had grabbed his phone and then headed into my living room. I can hear him softly talking now, though he'd closed the door and his voice is muffled.

I know I shouldn't eavesdrop, but I can't help it. I'm so curious about Ryder and who he's become over the years.

"...What's wrong?" he's asking with genuine concern. I've never heard him sound so sincerely worried for another person before, aside from his sister, but I can tell from the way he's talking that it's not Jade on the other end of the line. "Wait, where are you? You don't need to be alone. I'll come to you. Stay put. I'll be right there."

When he rushes back into the room and starts dragging on his clothes, I pretend not to have heard anything.

"I have to run out to help a friend," he says, hopping to the side as he wrestles with his pants.

I nod blankly, trying to process the bewildering storm of emotions inside of me and the fact that Ryder was leaving not even five minutes post hooking up with me. Was it another girl on the line? Had he gotten his fill and now he wanted to head onto his next conquest? That would be typical Ryder.

When he's pulled his shirt on, he moves over to me. He reaches out, brushing my hair back from my face.

I meet his eyes, hating how desperately I'm yearning for him to say something that will make me feel better... but he doesn't say a word.

His palm glides against my cheek one more time before he turns and rushes away. A second later, I hear the door slam.

Tears well in my eyes, even though I know I have no reason to feel upset. I'd said this was a one time only thing. I knew going into this how Ryder operates with women.

I have to tell myself this was for the best.

It was only one night, after all. One night can't change anything.

CHAPTER FIVE

# Ryder

I grip the steering wheel, my mind still back with Stella even as I zoom farther and farther down the street.

After running out of her home, I'd darted all the way back to the club to find my car. I hated leaving her like that, but when you get a call like the one I'd received, you have to get a move on.

When I'd looked into those golden eyes of Stells' before leaving, there were so many things I'd wanted to say. I'd wanted to tell her that it felt so right to be next to her, that no one else had ever made me feel like she had, that her lips were the only ones I wanted to kiss – but I'd never spoken like that to anyone before and my tongue failed me.

Plus, she and I had always been such fierce competitors with one another in our youth. She'd never seemed to like being around me. Was there any way Stella could've felt what I had?

In the end, I'd just bailed. Maybe I'll come up with the perfect words later.

All of a sudden, a hulking body stumbles out in front of my car.

With a grunt of surprise, I slam on the brakes and the car skids to a quick halt just a few inches in front of the stumbling figure. The bloke lurches forward, palms pressing into the front of my car.

"Oi!" I shout through the open window. "You lookin' to get hit?"

The man moves closer. In the headlights, Kai's face is illuminated.

His eyes are glassy from booze and I can all but smell the alcohol on him from inside my car. It was my rugby playing friend that had called, drunkenly ranting and raving in a voice so incoherent I could hardly hear him. At least he'd made himself easy to find.

I sigh, shaking my head. After parking, I climb out of the road. Kai staggers over toward me and I loop an arm around him.

"What happened, bro?" I mutter as I heft him into the backseat of my car.

He swallows hard, his face contorting with misery.

My best friend isn't one to drink himself silly, nor is he one to get emotional. He keeps his heart close to his sleeve, nearly to a fault.

"Was it your parents?" I press quietly. He looks like he might explode if he doesn't let something off his chest. "You were supposed to meet up with them, right?"

"...My mom didn't show," he croaks, slurring. "But my dad... he just sat there like a robot. He asked if anyone had knocked any bloody sense into me. If I'd decided to give up my foolish ambitions. If I was willing to be a part of my own family again or if I insisted on continuing to disgrace them..." Kai speaks in a deep replication of his father's condescending voice.

He goes limp, shaking his head. I sigh and sink down onto the seat beside him.

"With the way they're insisting on disregarding me, my parents might as well be dead, eh?" he continues before groaning loudly and smacking his head. "Hell, I shouldn't have said that to you Ryder."

I pat his leg and shrug, mustering up a smug grin that I'm sure would fool my drunk pal.

"You know I don't think about my parents' death much. I've got rugby and all the women in the world to drown my sorrows."

He chuckles and nods. "I wish I could be like you sometimes. I wish I could just forget about everything hurting me... and Jade..."

"Jade?" I repeat, confused about why Kai would be bringing up my little sister.

It doesn't seem like I'll be getting a response however, as Kai is starting to doze off.

At least I can let my smirk fade. It falls so quickly it's like I've ripped off a mask, which it might as well be.

It isn't true in the slightest that I've forgotten the pain of my parents' passing. I think about them every single day, but I know I have to be strong for Jade. I can't let my little sister see how much I still struggle with that loss.

I'd give anything to see Mum and Dad one more time, to spend five more minutes with them. I have Jade, and aside from rugby, she's my whole world... but I still have a hollowness inside of me that's only even slightly squelched when I'm chasing women.

Then there's Stella.

For a little while, I wasn't hollow. I was whole... and it only lasted as long as her arms were around me. Maybe that's all I have to tell her. Maybe those are the perfect words I was looking for.

Swallowing hard, I grab my phone and dial her number, praying she hadn't changed it since we were kids.

The line rings and rings until I'm about to give up hope when, suddenly, the line clicks.

"...Hello?" Stella murmurs. Her voice is tired and husky. It almost sounds like she was crying, though that wouldn't make sense. Was she sleeping?

"It's Ryder. I want to-"

"Remember when I said I would only be yours for a night?" she interjects frostily. "Let's keep it that way."

The line goes dead, but I'm frozen. I keep holding my cell to my ear, staring out through the dark night as Kai snores beside me.

All in one night, I'd found someone who might be able to heal me – and I'd managed to lose her too.

CHAPTER SIX

# Stella

"Stella...? Stella? Are you in there?"

I gulp, shooting back slightly from my desk and looking up into my concerned boss's face.

The middle-aged man folds his arms across his chest. "Are you feeling alright? You look pale. Actually, you've looked off all week."

"I've had a bit of a cold, but I think it's starting to let up," I answer hastily. My cheeks flush with embarrassed heat. "I'm so sorry for being distracted."

He sighs and shakes his head. "Don't worry about it. You're usually on top of your game. Why don't you head home early today?

Swing by somewhere and get some soup or something for yourself, eh?"

I give a hesitant nod. "Sure. I promise I'll be back to normal tomorrow."

When my boss leaves, I slowly stand up and gather my things. My head spins, little black dots swirling in front of my vision, but I shake my head to clear it. This bug of mine has certainly been stubborn. For the past few weeks, I've been struggling to keep food down and I've had some dizziness. I reckon it's the stress of trying to put Ryder behind me.

Telling him not to call me anymore had been the hardest thing I'd ever done... and nearly seven weeks has passed since then. I thought it'd get easier to forget him, but every day I wake up longing for him more.

I'd always been a fan of the Auckland rugby team, but I'd been unable to follow their progress lately. I know they went to New Plymouth and pummeled the Taranaki team and I also know that the National Cup was being hosted here soon, but I'd tried to keep my distance from anything related to Ryder since saying goodbye to him.

It was for my own good that we parted ways. It's not like he could ever change. To just keep longing for him would only cause me more pain in the long run, I'm sure of it.

After leaving the office, I wander down the road, letting the warm afternoon breeze ruffle my hair. Though the day is balmy and nice, an uncomfortable chill makes my teeth chatter. My eyelids feel so heavy that I can hardly keep them open, and even keeping my legs moving is proving to be impossible.

Maybe this wasn't just a cold?

Is there something wrong with me?

Staggering to the side, I sink down onto a bench and drop my head into my hands. I squeeze my eyes shut, trying to calm the panicking pace of my racing heart.

"Are you alright there?" someone asks from above me. "Wait, Stells? Is that you? I almost didn't recognize you, you look so rough."

I lift my head, my throat going tight when I see none other than Ryder looming over me. He has a teddy bear tucked under one arm along with a box of chocolates.

Gifts for a girl, no doubt. It makes my stomach turn even more. The last thing I want is his romantic life thrust in my face.

"Since when do you have a sweet tooth?" I whisper, trying to tease him, but as I force the words out, the whole world begins to pitch back and forth.

"You don't look good," he says worriedly, sinking down beside me onto the bench.

I feel the heat of his body washing over me, stealing my breath, just as my vision begins to go dark.

"Ryder..." I whisper.

My body sags to the side, his strong arms swooping around me.

"Stay with me, babe!" he cries desperately. "Stells, you're going to be okay... Stells?!"

My head lolls and the last things I see are his beautiful blue eyes before everything goes black.

# Ryder

Stella looks so fragile as she lays swathed in starched white hospital bed sheets that I can't stand to take my eyes off of her. Even blinking is difficult.

After the ambulance arrived, I'd lied and told them I was her boyfriend so that they'd let me stay with her. The whole ride out here, I'd clutched her hand... but her fingers were cold as ice.

It was hardly the reunion I would've wanted for the two of us.

For weeks, she's all I've been able to think about. I'd tried my best to forget her, but it's like life changed the moment I fell into her bed. No amount of partying or pretty girls could make me forget her. I'd hardly been able to touch a woman, it felt so wrong compared to how right it felt to have Stella in my arms.

And now, she's sick and there's nothing I can do to help her.

Softly, my fingertips brush against her face, following the smooth curve of her cool cheek.

"Open your eyes, Stells..." I whisper, leaning down to press a kiss against her clammy forehead.

This is almost too much for me to bear.

The beeping of the hospital machines, her pale face... it reminds me so much of the day I lost my parents.

Behind me, the door to Stella's hospital room swings open and a man shuffles inside.

"Hello," he greets me in a stern voice before stiffly shaking my hand. "I'm Dr. Morris. You're the significant other?"

I nod hastily. I don't care that I've lied, someone needs to be here with Stella. I won't let her wake up in this hospital room alone.

The doctor curtly nods his head. He flips through a file briefly, eyes skimming the pages.

"Am I to assume you're the father then?" he asks.

"Father?" I sputter, taking a stumbling step back. "Father to what?"

My heart has never raced so fast. It pounds against my ribs, the rapid sound nearly drowning out what the doctor was saying.

"...Erm, the baby..." he sighs, eyeing me uncertainly.

Gulping, I grip the side of the counter behind me and take a shuddering breath.

"I... I am," I whisper hoarsely.

I could be, after all... couldn't I? And if I said no or said I had no idea what he was talking about, would he have forced me to leave?

Am I a father? Is Stella carrying my child?

Pure, bone-chilling terror seeps through my veins... as does elation.

The thought of being a parent is something I'd never considered, but suddenly, it felt like the best choice of all.

Dr. Morris clears his throat. "Stella's levels show she's at nearly two months conception wise. I suspect it's a bad bout of dehydration that's brought her to us today. We've already got an IV with fluids running. We'll do a few more tests before she's able to be discharged. I'll be back around to check on her in a little bit."

"But she's going to be okay?" I ask urgently. "And the baby?"

For a moment, the man's severe expression softens. He reaches out and gently pats my shoulder.

"They're both going to be fine. Relax for a moment."

Still flustered, I nod and watch him go. Only once the door closes do I suck in a deep and rasping breath. My knees are shaking so much that I nearly collapse. I manage to stumble over to Stella's bedside, collapsing in the chair beside her where I'd been seated for at least an hour.

I grab her hand, drawing to my face as I press a kiss against her palm.

A baby. My baby.

Could it be?

Suddenly, Stella's fingers twitch. Gasping, I straighten and find her golden eyes cracking open. She gives a quiet whimper of fear as she looks around, unable to figure out where she is, but I gently cup her face in my hand and turn her to look at me. As soon as our eyes meet, she goes still.

"You're at the hospital, Stella, but you're safe. The doctor reckons you were dehydrated."

She wets her dry lips and slowly eases back against the bed. I stay close by, one hand at her cool cheek. She's still pale, but there's some color coming back to her lovely cheeks. It's such a relief to see her moving again that I would've danced around the room had I been willing to move an inch from her.

"And you've been here the whole time?" she asks, voice croaking slightly. "Since I passed out?"

My chin ducks in a nod. "The whole time, Stells. You weren't alone for an instant."

Her eyes search mine. I'm still leaning over her and our faces are so close that our noses almost brush.

"Ryder..." she murmurs. She bites her lip, looking conflicted. "I just... these last few weeks have been so-"

Again, the door to the hospital room creaks loudly open, cutting off Stella.

What had she been about to say? She'd looked so intent on whatever it would've been.

Dr. Morris strides back inside, looking pleased to see Stella awake.

"I noticed movement from outside the room window!" he says, his harsh doctorly voice sounding nearly cheerful. "Has your boyfriend filled you in on the diagnosis yet?"

"Boyfriend?" Stella sputters, jaw dropping as she looks at me and then the doctor. "Wait, diagnosis? You mean the dehydration?"

The doctor nods. "Yes, it's very common in the first trimester of pregnancy. You do need to make sure you keep your fluids at a healthy level for the baby, Stella."

CHAPTER EIGHT

# Stella

"Thank you, doctor," I choke out, trying not to look like I'm about to pass out again. "...If we could just have a moment."

My head is spinning, thoughts and questions whirling so fast inside my head that my skull is probably bruised.

"Certainly," the white-coated man responds.

Once the doctor is out of the room, I whirl toward Ryder. Ryder gazes at me, a hesitant smile curving his handsome mouth, but I'm in no mood for smiles right now.

"You told them you were my boyfriend?" I hiss angrily.

The smile is immediately wiped off his face. He appraises me, scrutinizing my furious expression as though he doesn't understand the fact that he violated my privacy.

"I didn't want you to be alone, Stells. That's the only reason I said that. They wouldn't let me stick around if I was just some random bloke."

That's the only reason he stayed by my side? Because he was worried I'd be a little lonely waking up in a hospital bed? That hits my already wounded ego hard. I grit my teeth and fold my arms.

"I'll help you with the baby too," he continues hastily. He's trying to placate me, but it's only making me more livid. "Money or whatever you need. I'll give you anything."

Scoffing, I shoot him a withering glare. "I don't need anything from you, Ryder. Neither does this baby. We're not a charity case. And besides... it's not your child. I can tell you that with 100% certainty."

Ryder blinks a few times, the significance of my words registering syllable by syllable.

Is that disappointment filling his blue eyes? But why? Why would playboy, perpetual bachelor Ryder want to be tied down with a child? It doesn't make any sense. He's not any more cut out to be a father than he is a boyfriend.

That's why I have to do this. That's why I have to lie.

Ryder doesn't understand what it means to put other people before yourself. He doesn't understand what it would mean to be a parent. I have to keep this secret. I won't pressure him into being something he isn't.

"You have someone else, Stells?" he asks.

He looks and sounds so distraught that I'm not sure what to think, but every inch of me is exhausted, and I've just received the biggest shock of my life. My head is pounding and my heart is throbbing and I need some time alone to process this.

"No. The father is... he's out of the picture already."

One second, I'm just trying to nurse a broken heart and the next I suddenly have to prepare myself to be a mother. I've always known I wanted to be a mum, but I'd expected to plan it... I hadn't expected it to happen because of a one-night stand with a man terrified of commitment.

As much as I say it's not Ryder's, it can only be his. I hadn't been with anyone else in months.

"You need to go," I repeat quietly. "All that I need is to be on my own. I can do this on my own. I'm happy on my own."

I can tell by the stubborn look on his face that the wants to argue, but instead of saying anything, he slowly stands up. He walks to the doorway, turning one more time to look at me as he gathers the gifts he'd purchased for some other girl off the counter. Then, like a shadow, he vanishes over the threshold.

For the second time, I'm forced to watch Ryder leave while internally screaming for him to return.

Am I making the right choice for all of us? Or have I just made the worst decision of my life?

CHAPTER NINE

# Ryder

Sweat drenches my jersey as our coach grabs me and gives me a shake.

I try to catch my breath, shaking my head to get my damp, dark hair out of my eyes.

"Where's your head at, Ryder? You can't be bothered to concentrate? It's the National Cup!" he cries in frustration. "You're a dozen steps behind everyone else!"

My chest heaves as I dully look over my shoulder at the field. We're in the final minutes of the game and it's completely tied up. I know I should be giving it my best shot, but all I want to do right now is return to Stella. It kills me that she's here somewhere here in Auckland going through what must be the hardest time of her life.

It's been days since I last saw her, but she hasn't faded from my thoughts for an instant.

I don't care if I'm not the father of her child. I don't care who is. All I know is that I want to be at her side. I want to make things better. I know I messed up at the hospital, but what can I do to fix things?

She's managed to steal my heart and I haven't even had the strength to tell her as much. Would that only push her further away? Or would she finally see how sincere I am about her?

"Oi!" gasps Kai as he rushes over to me.

He gives me nudge in the ribs, but his eyes are concerned. "What's going on with you, bro? You've been totally out of it lately. What's going on?"

"I bet it's a girl," pants Gray as he jogs up toward us. We don't have long before we have to return to the field, and I'm not really in the mood for even their friendly banter. "What, did you finally get rejected by someone, Ryder?"

I want to put my smug mask back on. I want to laugh loudly and joke around and torment my teammates right back... but I just don't have it in me anymore. I've never had a problem faking my snide sarcasm, but I'm so drained that I barely have the strength even to be on this field.

Kai grasps my shoulder, frowning at me. "I can tell something's seriously wrong, bro. Screw the game. If you need to let something out, we're here for you. Aren't we?"

He looks around at the rest of the team. The lot of them pauses for a moment, seeming to realize simultaneously that I'm not just pouting over something... that my heart is crumbling in my chest.

"We can't risk losing the game," I mutter, but Jax strides forward and grasps my other shoulder.

"It's about more than the game. It's about family. Isn't that what you always say?" he says.

My eyes shift around each of them, stunned by how much they all care. I've never felt so lucky to be on the Auckland team. I doubted any of the other rugby teams had the same sense of brotherhood we do. Maybe that's why we're doing so well so far.

Then, from over Manu's shoulder... I see her.

Stella is in the stands, standing near one of the entryways like she'd only just come in to watch the last few minutes of the game. Her face is somber and conflicted.

As soon our eyes meet and I lurch instinctively toward her, Coach starts signaling us all to get back on the field.

I know my job is to play this game, but I just can't do it. If I were to turn my back on Stella again, I would never forgive myself. I'd left her twice, and a third time isn't something I'm willing to do.

The blokes on my team follow my stare, noting Stella. Even though I don't say anything, it's clear to everyone that whatever is going on with us involves her too.

"Go get your girl," Kai whispers in my ear. "We can handle the game."

"That's right!" says Gray, pounding one fist into his palm. "We'll get the Cup. You get your lady!"

The rest of the men grin and nod. Even the coach gives a groan.

"I tell you what, Ryder. If this is real, then I'll do whatever I can to stall," says Coach. "This isn't just one of your flings, is it?"

I shake my head, swallowing hard. "If this is real, I won't have any more flings, Coach."

His face softens. He nods and winks before marching up to one of the referees.

Turning, I take off across the field toward Stella as surprise soars across her face.

I had to learn the hard way that when you care about someone, you take every chance to tell them that. You never know how short life can be. I've let my fear of getting too close to people I could lose control me for far too long.

Now is my chance to tell Stella exactly what she means to me, and I won't waste the opportunity for another second.

CHAPTER TEN

# Stella

As Ryder runs across the field in my direction, those sexy rugby shorts leaving very little to the imagination as they ride up his long, muscled legs, I can't help but glance over my shoulder like he'd be barreling toward someone who happened to be behind me... but no, there's just a wall there.

My heart pulses, palms going clammy.

What am I going to say to him?

I hadn't intended to cause a scene. I'd been hoping to just quietly slip into the stadium as the match was finishing.

Over the last few days, my guilt had taken over. I just couldn't keep this secret from

Ryder. He had to know that he was the father of my child... even if he'd never be able to forgive me for lying. He'd already lost his parents, he didn't need to lose the chance to be a father too. It wouldn't be fair of me to keep him in the dark.

"Stella!" he cries, panting as he skids to a stop at the edge of the field.

He holds out an arm toward me and I can't stop myself from rushing forward, grabbing hold of his outstretched hand. Our fingers lace automatically together.

"You came," he murmurs. He's breathless, but a smile plays on his mouth. "I guess you didn't get enough of me, eh?"

A weak laugh escapes my throat. I'd so missed that sarcastic humor of Ryder's... but now I feel even more guilty than I did before. I'd pushed him away so coldly, and now he was holding my hand and smiling at me – and I'd even interrupted one of the biggest rugby matches of his career.

What had I been thinking when I decided to come out here?

"Stells," he says, squeezing my hand before I could even think of trying to escape. "I just need to tell you one thing. I'm done with-"

"I lied," I croak out. My whole body is shaking, even my voice is quivering. I know he's about to tell me he's done with me, but I need to get this out first. That way, if this conversation is our last, at least he knows the truth. "The baby. It's yours. I know lying about that is unforgivable but I just... I was scared. I wasn't thinking straight. I was shocked."

I brace myself, waiting for him to grow furious. Instead, Ryder gently reaches up and cups my face.

"I understand fear, Stells. Believe me... what I was about to say is that I'm done being a playboy. I'm done with that whole act. I was so afraid of letting people get close after I lost my parents that I filled that hole in my heart with senseless intimacy. Physically, I felt better for a minute, but emotionally... I was broken. Until you and I got together a few weeks back. I want to be with you, Stella. I want to be your partner, both in love and in fathering our child. I never want you to be alone."

Tears pool in my eyes, slipping down my face. "I want that too, Ryder."

"Ryder!" cries a tiny voice.

A little girl suddenly rushes up, dragging a familiar-looking teddy bear along the ground. She looks at me shyly and then at the rugby player.

"Manu says you need to hurry back! Mr. Coach can't hold off for long!" she says. Urgency makes her tiny voice shrill.

"I'll just be a second longer," Ryder promises her, ruffling her hair.

The girl peeks at me from over the head of her stuffed bear.

"...Was that a present from Ryder?" I ask hesitantly, gesturing at the toy.

Brightening, the little girl nods. "Yes! Her name is Mrs. Fluff! Ryder comes and plays with me and my bears all the time. We have so much fun... maybe you can come too? My name is Rosie!"

Someone calls the little girl's name and she glances over her shoulder, rushing back toward another woman nearby, a woman wearing an Auckland jersey with Manu's number on it.

"That bear was a gift for that little girl?" I whisper, startled. When I'd seen him with that bear, I'd assumed he was trying to woo another woman.

He nods. "Manu's got some new ladies in his life. I wanted to make them feel welcome."

Turning toward him, I smile softly. This whole time, I'd thought it was impossible for Ryder to change, when in reality, he'd been changing from the beginning. It was me who refused to see it.

Now that my eyes were opened, I could see Ryder perfectly. He was flawed, but he was good, and I'd been falling for him since the moment we met up at that bar.

"Go win that Cup for us, Ryder. Then you and I can have more than one thing to celebrate, eh?"

"For you, babe," he muses. His smile spreads radiantly across his face. "Anything. If you can wait five more minutes for me to trounce these blokes, I'll never make you wait for me again."

I laugh as he again takes off just as both teams return to the field.

The rest of the game is an intense one and the ball flies back and forth between the teams until, finally, Ryder scores the winning point.

The stadium erupts as the Auckland boys cheer and tackle one another joyously. One last time, Ryder breaks away from them and rushes toward me. This time, he dashes up the stairs so that he can scoop me up into his arms.

As he holds me close, one hand on my belly, I can feel his heart beating with not only the excitement of the big victory, but over our future too.

"From here on out, Stells," he says gently, eyes blazing into mine. "We're a family, and family is the most important thing."

EPILOGUE

# Ryder

I close my eyes so that I can savour the gentle music filling the air.

The delicate harp notes being plucked now are so different from the raucous nightclub tunes I used to dance to, but I don't miss it at all. My life might have taken a few changes since then... but I couldn't be happier.

The music changes and my eyes open so that I can look down the aisle.

All around me are Stella and I's friends and family.

Little Rosie is making her way forward, giggling as she carefully throws rose petals from a basket.

Kai and Jade stand on either side of me, stealing glances at one another across the aisle and blushing. Jax and Gray and Coach are in the audience, along with some very special ladies of their own as well. Over this last rugby season, so much has changed for all of us – and it's all been for the better. We've all grown closer and stronger, and now we even had the National Cup to call our own.

Manu, waiting for Rosie nearby, deftly holds a three-month-old infant in his arms. He brings the baby closer to me so that I can grin down at my son. Born perfectly healthy and right on time, the little boy has my bright blue eyes and Stella's golden locks.

Baby Noah is going to be a looker just like his dad, if I do say so myself.

"Your mum is almost here," I promise him, stroking his tiny face. Noah coos and grabs at my hand, clutching my pinky, and my heart melts in my chest.

Being a father is everything I imagined it would be. Spending every day with Stella and Noah is my own version of Heaven.

Reaching the end of the aisle, Rosie giggles and rushes to Manu, clinging to his leg as she beams out at all of us.

Then, at the end of the aisle, the most beautiful woman I've ever seen appears.

Stella walks forward slowly, clutching her bouquet. A lace veil dances over her shoulders as she glides forward. Her cheeks glow pink. When she reaches me, she passes her bouquet to Jade, who leans over to kiss her cheek and give her a hug. When Stella turns back toward me, she blows a kiss toward Noah.

"Do you take this man to be your lawful husband?" the officiant asks, turning to Stella.

"I do," Stella responds immediately. "With my whole heart, I do."

The man looks at me. "And you do take this woman to be your lawful wife?"

I reach toward her, gathering her hands in my own. I kiss the backs of her palms, smiling at her. "I absolutely do."

"Then I now pronounce you husband and wife!" the officiant says as the people sitting out in pretty white chairs begin to cheer wildly.

I sweep Stella forward into my arms, dipping her backward as my lips find hers. We kiss deeply before straightening. Stella reaches forward to take Noah, cuddling our baby against her as I wrap them both up in my arms.

"I love you," I murmur into her ear. "Every day I love you more. You've given me peace of heart and mind, you've given me joy, you've given me hope. Stella, you and Noah are my world. You will be forever."

"I love you too, Ryder," she murmurs. Tears glisten in her eyes. "When we were kids, I never would've imagined the man you've become... but you've helped me become a better woman too. I love you eternally, and I'm so happy that we've found one another."

Gently, I tighten my embrace around my wife and my son, kissing Noah's forehead and Stella's lips once more.

It's amazing how much can change in a single year... but every rough and difficult moment was worth it because it brought Stella into my arms. Together, I'm sure we can help carry one another through good times and through bad, and I never intend to let go of her hand again.

The End

# LIAM

# Liam

My eyes drift around the crowded table as I numbly take in the sound of laughing rugby players, the grins on their faces as bright as the excitement gleaming in their eyes.

The young rugby stars are at their prime, ready to take on the world – or at least the National Cup tournament. Afterward, a few lucky ones will end up selected for the Blues squad, and then eventually make their way to the All Blacks. My time as their coach will have come to an end. But I reckon they're not thinking about that. This lot are thinking about the Cup and what it will take to win it and how their careers will explode if they manage to take that trophy into their strong and eager clutches.

To them, they're teetering at the cusp of greatness. The future is almost in their grasp.

They don't know yet how easy it is for life to flip upside down without warning.

I'd been young and energetic once. I'd had fans chant my name. I'd strode across that field, veins throbbing with exhilaration and my gaze locked on the National Cup. One rough tumble knocked the wind from those sails before I could bloody comprehend that I'd cost us the win, or that my career as a player was over.

"Coach!" Jax says, reaching closer to clap me on the shoulder. "You daydreaming over there?"

I blink hard and grin at the zealous player before folding my arms over my chest and allowing a smirk to settle on my face. "I was thinking about our next drills. You lot are in for a killer workout, that's for sure."

Jax just laughs, always eager for more practice. The hardest working player on the team, aside from perhaps Manu, Jax is prepared for anything when it comes to rugby.

"Cheers, boys!" howls Ryder from across the table. He lifts his pint of beer, amber liquid sloshing over the side of it. A cold river of beer streams down onto the table. "This season is going to be the one that changes everything!"

Everyone lifts their glasses, clinking them together before drinking deeply.

The small and slightly dingy restaurant is bustling tonight. The eatery is filled with the sound of plates clinking and patrons chatting and a cook barking commands in the back. I'd offered to take the team somewhere nicer but they'd insisted on coming to this tiny bistro.

Apparently, according to Kai and Ryder at least, it offered the coldest beer in town. If I had to guess, they only wanted to come here because they wouldn't have to change out of their rugby uniforms first. We'd headed straight over after another intense practice.

Soon, we'll be the winners of the National Cup... or we'll be losers.

Every season, that tournament is a painful reminder of just how close I got to the trophy back in the day.

Jax. Kai. Manu. Gray. Ryder. They're my all-stars, the ones I'd recruited personally to the team.

There are others on the team, but those five are the ones who mean the most to me. I'm not a sentimental man, but by now, I thought I'd have a family. These young men are as close as I may ever get to that. I'm trying to imprint every moment I can to my memory so I never forget how it felt to be their coach.

"G'day, babe," Ryder purrs. He takes another slurp of his beer and winks at the young waitress who's approached the table. "Ain't you a sight for sore eyes, eh?"

At first, I can't be bothered to even look over to see who our most flirtatious teammate is ogling now, though I can tell by the raucous laughter at the table that she must not have been impressed.

The blue-eyed athlete begins to pout. Ryder isn't used to being brushed off by the ladies. He may be cheesy, but he has a way with the women that even I don't understand. At least he might be single as long as I am.

"Your waiter had to run out, so I'll be picking up the table," the girl explains politely. Her voice is sweet and bubbly.

I shift in my seat, leaning around Jax so I can get a glimpse of the waitress. My eyes skim over a tight black skirt that inches down plump, tan thighs. I've never seen a waitressing outfit look so damn good before.

"My name is Ava," continues the young woman. She must be fresh out of uni. Her eyes, dark and rich as chestnuts, crinkle in the corners when she smiles. "Is there anything I can do for you...?" She trails off when she catches me gazing at her, pure shock registering in those dazzling eyes of hers.

"You bet I do-" Ryder starts to say before his best friend on the team shoves a well-timed elbow into Ryder's ribs.

"What the hell, Kai?" hisses Ryder with another wounded scowl.

Kai smirks and shakes his head. "I think we're good to go. It's about time we head out. Right, boys?"

The others give a murmur of agreement. It's late, after all, and we had a long day of practice. Sharply, Ava sucks in a sudden breath and musters another smile to her face.

"I'll get the bill then," she murmurs. Her gaze collides with mine one more time before she stumbles backward and hurries off.

There was something in the way that girl looked at me... I can't explain it, but suddenly I feel as if I'm a fish snagged on a hook. Every step away she takes threatens to yank me after her.

"One sec, boys," I state quietly. I push back from the table to climb to my feet.

I don't know what I want to say, or even what I want from her, but I just know I can't let her out of my sight just yet.

"Get it, Coach!" Ryder hollers as I pursue the young waitress.

He's still rubbing his side, but he's more interested in me chasing down the cute girl than the bruises on his rib.

I find Ava by the register, her back to me as she hastily rolls clean silverware in fresh towels. Is it my imagination, or are her fingers trembling?

"Excuse me," I murmur, fishing in my pocket for my wallet and producing a credit card. "I'm sorry about Ryder. I reckon he can come off a little... unruly," I sigh. "I'd like to put all of the table's meals on my check."

When I speak, her entire body freezes. Her chest rises sharply as she inhales. For a moment, she simply stares forward away from me, but then, only inches at a time, she hesitantly turns.

The entire time, I'm dying to get another good look at her.

I want to gaze into those eyes. I want to memorize the curve of her lips. The languidness with which she moves is torturous.

I've known beautiful women... but none of them have ever made me feel this intense and sudden longing like Ava has.

The movement sends dark curls tumbling over her shoulders. She wets her lips as she gazes at me, her nostrils flared, eyes hooded, pupils dilated.

"Liam King," she gasps.

Her melodic voice sends a shockwave of pleasure through me.

"You already know me?" I murmur curiously.

"How could I not?" Her gorgeous mouth opens, revealing the tip of a perfectly pink tongue as she struggles to say something further, but her words fail her.

She brushes her hair back, pressing her palm to her cheek as her eyes search mine.

That's perfectly fine. She doesn't have to speak anymore. I know the look on her face well.

It's enough to make every muscle inside me instantly tense.

The air between us crackles as pulsing energy throbs between her body and mine. When I breathe, I can taste her fragrance over the scent of greasy burgers and frying fish.

Ava is beautiful, sweet, and young.

Hell, she's young enough that she could be my daughter.

It might be wrong, but I've never wanted anyone more than I want her.

## CHAPTER TWO

# Ava

My heart pulses so fast I can hardly catch my breath. It hammers my ribs harder than a battering ram.

Liam King is really standing in front of me. The former star of the Auckland team and now the coach. He's singlehandedly leading Auckland straight to the National Cup – and he's so close that my clammy, trembling palms could reach out and brush against his toned chest if I had any less restraint.

He's even more handsome in person than he is on TV. I can so vividly remember my father cheering for Liam while wearing his Auckland fan jersey. Even though Dad died years ago, I'm struck with the fresh urge to call him and tell him that Liam King – *the* Liam King – is here.

If I wasn't so shell-shocked, I would've asked for Liam's autograph.

When I just stare blankly at him, he asks "You all good?" a husky, rich voice that makes sweat form on the back of my neck.

"Of course," I stammer, mustering a smile and hoping my coffee-colored cheeks don't burn too crimson.

Liam just nods, hardly blinking as he watches me. It might be unprofessional, but I can't stop my eyes from sweeping up and down his burly figure. I reckon he's all I'm going to be dreaming about for weeks now.

I step behind the register and take his card, knocking it against the machine at least twice because my hands are shaking so much. It's not just my hands though. My entire body is shaking. I have to press my knees together hard to keep my legs from collapsing beneath me.

Finally, I swipe his credit card. For my dad, I even give Liam a healthy little discount.

"The team's doing amazing this season," I add as the computer deliberates over the payment. "I watch all the games. I can't wait to see you all pulverize Taranaki when you head to New Plymouth."

He chuckles and nods, accepting the card when I hand it over before scribbling his signature down on the receipt. I stare at it longingly, wishing I could work up the nerve to ask him to sign something for me.

It's blowing my mind that, of all the fancy places in Auckland, Liam would bring his team here. We're a tiny joint mostly suited to the drunk people stumbling out of nearby bars in the middle of the night. I don't even want to be here, so I'm not sure why Liam would either.

One day soon, I'm going to be out of here. I've been saving up to open my own bakery for over a year. When I'm not waiting tables, I'm slaving over my oven trying to whip up tasty confections. I'd even put in my two weeks' notice already with the hope that I'll be able to land on my feet. I'm sick of smelling like chips and beer. My dad's last advice to me had been to take more risks. Plus, I'd been taking online and phone orders for a while now and had a decent side gig going.

When he hands over the signed receipt, our fingers brush. My stomach drops, fireworks exploding through my veins. My lashes flutter, bursts of crimson rocking against the backs of my eyelids.

He says something that I can't hear over the loud beating of my heart.

By the time I'm gripping the counter and able to see past the swirling dots of my vision, Liam has turned away from me.

His broad shoulders sway beneath the fluorescent restaurant lights as he walks away. My lips part, tongue clicking against the roof of my mouth as I desperately try to come up with something to say that will keep him in front of me. I'm not ready for him to walk away yet. I'm not ready to say goodbye.

As if reading my mind, the Auckland coach swivels back toward me.

"If I can..." he begins, before my cell suddenly starts shrieking from my back pocket.

Now I know I'm turning red. I usually silence my phone at work, but it must've slipped my mind this time.

With a gasp, I snatch my phone and hurriedly try to silence it, but the moment's evaporated.

"I'll see you around, Ava," Liam says simply. He winks, a movement that makes my battering ram of a heart turn into a catapult.

He remembered my name. I think I might be able to die happy now.

I watch him go, eyes following his long back and strong legs. My throat goes tight. All those young guys might look great in their uniforms, but there's something about Liam, mature and wise and tall Liam, that makes heat flood through me.

When my phone buzzes again, I lift it dazedly to my cheek.

"Hello," I whisper into the receiver of my phone.

My ear is met with a barking, gruff voice that makes me wince.

"Ava," my ex-boyfriend grunts immediately. Compared to Liam's silky tenor, Brady's manner of speaking feels like sandpaper. "Babe. You know breaking up with me was a mistake. I'm the best thing you'll ever have, eh? Let me come round later. I'll show you what you're missing out on."

Instead of answering, I just lower the phone. I whip toward Liam's table, only to find it empty. Every one of the Auckland players is gone, including the coach.

I'd had my chance with Liam, and now it was gone.

## CHAPTER THREE

# Liam

The sun blazes, a perfect golden sphere in the sky. Every time I move, shouting at the team to repeat their drills in agonizing succession, my shirt sticks to my toned body. Beads of sweat glide down my back, doing little to offer relief.

By the end of practice, my knee is throbbing as I set my hands on my hips and grin out at the breathless, sweaty players. It's not just them I push to the limit. I have to push myself too. Though my knee had given out on me just before the National Cup in my youth, I still run alongside my men as much as I can. I need to be right beside them to help them train to be at their best.

"That was a bloody awesome practice, Coach!" pants Manu. He's partially doubled over, hands on his thick-as-tree-trunk thighs. He gasps, trying to catch his breath.

Beside him, Gray chuckles and mutters, "Suck up!"

"Shush, newbie!" Ryder wheezes with his trademark smirk.

"Are we going to get in one more practice tomorrow morning before we fly out to New Plymouth?" asks Jax. "If we don't beat Taranaki, we're out of the tournament. We're so close to winning the National Cup!"

I arch an eyebrow, impressed by the young man's gusto. I reckon it really shouldn't be a surprise though, seeing as Jax is aiming to be one of the youngest All Blacks players.

"Our flight out is at like five in the morning!" wails Ryder. "Are you bloody serious, bro?"

Jax smirks and shrugs. "Just trying to make sure we make get that Cup. Right, Coach?"

I laugh and clap his shoulder. "Yeah, no. I admire your willingness, Jax, but rest is just as important as practice... and so is a little fun."

"Fun?" Gray echoes, perking up and sharing a grin with Ryder. Those two were as continuously ready for pleasure as Jax and Manu were to train.

My chin dips in a curt nod. "That's right! Tonight, we're celebrating the fact that we're going to go pulverize the Taranaki team. I've arranged some food and drink to be dropped off. Breathe. Relax. Chat. Tomorrow, it's back to business."

While the rest of the team lets out a wild cheer, I don't miss Manu's slightly strained expression. It must be odd, even for him, to go home again after so long. He'd almost joined the Taranaki team before I convinced him to play for Auckland instead.

"Pulverize them, eh?" echoes Kai. "I've never heard you say something like that, Coach."

My mind briefly flickers back to the beautiful young waitress at the restaurant. It'd been a week or so since that night, though I'd thought of Ava daily since then. I'd even considered dropping by the restaurant just to see her again, but with the National Cup coming up, I know I need to focus on it. No distractions.

I clear my throat and shrug. "You lot head over and get some grub. The food is set out on tables by my office. I'll be right behind you."

The men laugh and wander away, tugging at their sweat-drenched jerseys.

I lift my hand, shielding the sun off my face when I spot something strange in the distance. A huge cake wobbles as it's being carried across the pavement.

"What the hell?" I chuckle as I jog across the field.

I hadn't ordered a cake, but whoever is carrying it must be tiny. The cake dwarfs them as it towers up into the sky.

"Let me take that," I offer hastily, scooping the cake up from the tan arms of whoever was carrying it.

"Thank you!" gushes a feminine voice.

The sound is so familiar that I almost drop the cake.

I hastily lower the cake, staring around it to find the beautiful, dark-haired young waitress from the restaurant.

Am I bloody dreaming?

"It's you," Ava gasps. Her eyes squeeze shut and then open wide. She's just as shocked as I am. "I didn't... the person who put in the order didn't say this was for the Auckland team! I figured it was just some junior league party."

The cake smells so delectable that my mouth is already watering, and I'm not one for desserts. Or maybe it's the sight of the gorgeous girl that's whet my appetite.

"My sister was in charge of ordering food for the team, she must've thought we needed something sweet," I explain.

"Oh." Ava curls one dark lock of wavy hair around her finger. "Um... I didn't get the chance to say so the other night but-"

"Oi!" someone crassly shouts. A moment later, some beefed up bloke storms forward across the hot pavement of the parking lot.

Instinctively, I shift between Ava and his looming figure.

"Will you hurry up, girl?" the man hisses, ignoring me completely. "I've been sitting in the car waiting for, like, ten minutes already. I can't be bothered to wait around for you all day!"

"I'm sure ten minutes must feel like an awful long time to someone like you," I mutter, irritated that anyone would speak to Ava like that.

The man narrows his beady eyes on me, fingers curling into fists. "You got something you want to say, bro? I know who you are. You're just some old man who lost his team the National Cup back in the day. Everyone knows you're just going to make Auckland lose again."

"Brady!" gasps Ava. "Shut up!"

"You're going to tell me what to do too?" he snaps back.

"That's enough," I snarl. Holding the cake easily in one hand, I wedge myself again between them. "I won't have you speaking to Ava that way. Get out of here unless you want a hiding. Got it?"

"I drove her," he hisses, spitting at the ground between my feet. "Come on, Ava. We're done here."

Ava's fingers curl against my shirt, not caring that I was still damp from the hard work out. She clings to me as though drawing strength from my hulking form, which I'm all too content with.

"No," she whispers, voice quivering slightly. "Liam is right. You need to go, Brady. It was a mistake to think we could work things out. I don't want to see you anymore – I *won't* see you anymore. Don't bother calling. Consider yourself blocked."

He glowers at her, his mouth opening as though he wanted to insult her again. When I shift so that I'm back in his line of vision, he slowly clamps his lips together. He glowers at me one more time before turning and storming off again.

"Coach, is everything okay?" Jax calls as he approaches. "We heard some guy shouting."

I nod and hold out the cake, allowing Jax to take it.

Ava is still clinging to me, her eyes directed toward that guy's car as it pulls out of the lot and heads away. She's stranded here.

"I'm going to escort this young lady safely home," I say, nodding at Jax. "You lot have fun tonight, but make sure no one has too much fun, eh? Remember the early flight."

Jax nods. He takes the cake, glancing between Ava and me before turning and heading back to the team.

I turn toward Ava and her hand slowly releases me, though I'm dying for her to touch me again. She gazes up at me, biting her lip.

"You don't have to do that, Liam. I'm sure I can find someone to pick me up."

I shake my head. "If he's waiting at your flat for you, he needs some sense knocked into him. I want to make sure you stay safe."

Ava's cheeks glow a delicate pink. "Actually... I'm kind of between places at the moment. I've been crashing on my friend's couch."

A frown tugs at the corners of my lips. "After having that guy go off on you like that, you need a bed, Ava. How about you take mine? I don't mind the couch."

Like a rose blooming, the flush of her cheeks deepens to a rich shade of scarlet.

Without hesitating a moment, the young woman nods.

## CHAPTER FOUR

# Ava

The elevator chimes merrily as the doors close, leaving Liam and I alone as the lift lurches upward.

We haven't spoken much since leaving the parking lot of the rugby field, which is honestly a relief. I don't want to explain what I was thinking when it came to dating Brady. Being involved with him was a big mistake, one I don't intend to ever repeat. After we broke up, he'd made a big deal about us still being friends and offered to help me make deliveries. I now realize that he just wanted to keep an eye on me.

"This was really kind of you," I murmur when the silence stretches on a bit too long. "My new lease doesn't pick up until Monday."

He shrugs his massive shoulders. He turns slightly toward me, kind eyes pouring into mine.

"It's all good. I didn't realize you were a baker. I'm pretty bummed I didn't get a taste of that cake. It looked delicious."

Giddy delight bubbles up in me at the compliment. "I'm opening my own bakery sometime soon. That's why I had to cut my other flat rental short. I needed a cheaper place."

His brow lifts slightly. "That's amazing, Ava. Really."

"I mean, you've done amazing things too," I answer shyly. "Look at how far Auckland has come this season. That's all because of you, Liam."

The doors of the elevator glide open and we step out into the hall.

"...Do you live alone?" I ask hesitantly. "I'm not intruding on anyone else, am I?"

He chuckles softly and shakes his head, digging into his pocket for his key. "Nope. Just me. Rugby has always been my priority. Everything else has fallen to the wayside."

His voice trails off into a sigh as he turns the key and pushes the door open. He steps back, allowing me to walk in first. I glance around curiously, noting the clean and well-kept space. On the walls are clippings of articles about the Auckland team as well as team photos. It's nice... but there's something distinctly lonely about it.

I can understand that. After my dad passed, I felt like I had no one to cling to, no one to point me in the right direction when it came to life. I was always floundering from one minute to the next. It was only when I decided to pursue baking that I finally felt like my feet had hard ground beneath them again.

"Can I make you some tea or anything? Coffee? You hungry?" he asks as he moves around the apartment, pulling a blanket and a pillow from a closet and tossing them at his admittedly comfy looking couch.

I shake my head, definitely not wanting to be a bother, when there's a sudden, loud knock on the door. Before either of us can even move, there's another loud bang. Again and again, something brutally pummels the wooden door.

"Ava!" shouts Brady's in his unmistakably rude voice. "I saw you go in there with that bloke! Don't make me bust this bloody door down!"

Mortification floods my veins.

"I am so sorry-" I cry out, but Liam just gently grips my arms and gives me a comforting squeeze.

"Don't you apologize for that ass's actions, eh? This is the whole reason I brought you here, so that if he pulled something like this, I could protect you. Take a seat and let me deal with him."

Tears well in the corners of my eyes but I nod. I hadn't had anyone look out for me like this in so long that I wasn't even entirely sure how to react.

Liam grabs his cell, shooting off a quick text before heading to the door of his apartment. He cracks it open just enough to glower down into Brady's face.

"You'll want to get out of here, bro," he growls. "Security is on their way. They don't take kindly to people like you causing a ruckus – and I've seen enough of you for a lifetime."

"Ava is my girl!" Brady shouts back nastily. "Ava! I know you're in there. Get your ass out here-"

Brady gives a curt cry as Liam strides out the door, grabbing him by the collar and pushing him against the hallway wall.

"You will not speak to her like that. Hell, you won't bloody speak to her ever again. You hear me?" snarls Liam. "She already told you she's done. Now get out of here!"

If Brady were a dog, he'd be cowering with his tail between his legs. He gives a childish whimper and scuttles backward when Liam releases him. At the same time, the elevator doors glide open again.

"Sorry, Mr. King," the security officer exiting the lift says. "At the door he said he knew you and your guest. It won't happen again."

Liam just shakes the officer's hand and shrugs, though he glowers at Brady one more time.

"Oi. You're lucky they got here when they did. Next time, I promise you there'll be no luck left."

Brady gulps, nodding as the security guard pulls him into the elevator. When the doors shut once more, Liam sighs and turns back to face me where I'm peeking out the apartment's door.

He hurries back toward me, gently brushing his hand against my arm.

"Are you alright, Ava?" he asks worriedly.

To even my own surprise, I start to laugh. I giggle until the tears welling in my eyes slip down my cheeks. The concern on his face grows stronger.

"I'm sorry... he's just been such a terror since I broke up with him. He's always calling, always showing up insisting to escort me on my bakery runs... and you almost made him cry, Liam! It's just hilarious – but in all honesty, thank you. I think I'm finally free of him."

"I know you are," He answers with a chuckle.

With a surprisingly soft touch, he brushes away my tears. A shiver rolls up my back and I have to bite my lip. The way he touches me... it sends sparks through my veins.

His thumb slowly traces the curve of my bitten lip and I slowly move closer to him, head tipping back so I can gaze into his eyes.

"Liam..." I whisper, heart beginning to pound against my ribs.

When I say his name, a soft growl escapes his throat. His other arm slips around my waist, pulling me against him. I melt easily against his chest, leaning up onto my tiptoes so I can be closer to him. His mouth descends on mine, capturing my lips.

My head spins, my body going limp in Liam's strong arms as his tongue boldly dances with my own.

This is easily the most moving, stirring kiss I've ever had in my life. I cling to Liam. Every place that our bodies touch is electrified.

"I've never felt this before," I gasp out, overwhelmed by the lust rooting deep in my body. "...I've never wanted anyone like this."

He lifts me, carrying me to the bedroom. We collapse on his bed, our mouth crashing again as we tear at one another's clothes. He takes his time undressing me, pulling my shirt over my head and greedily kissing every inch of skin he can find.

I writhe beneath him, begging for him to strip me fully. Desire throbs through every inch of me. It overpowers my senses, leaving me blindly thirsting for Liam.

He crawls over top of me once we've ripped each other's clothes off. My chest heaves, red lust glowing on the backs of my eyelids. We roll across the sheets, clinging to one another. My fingers rake down his back, my voice rising in fervent pitch.

I'm so desperate for him that I can't contain myself. I've become some primal, feral version of myself that I didn't even know existed.

He pins me down, mouth ravishing mine, before thrusting inside of me. My back arches, head thrown back against this pillow as we rock together. His hand knots in my hair so that he can kiss down my throat and my legs wrap tight around his hips, dragging him against me. The bed squeaks and groans beneath us as it desperately tries to withstand the forceful rock of our bodies.

When I'm sure I can take it no more, he buries himself inside of me one last time. Pleasure explodes in my core, sending wave after wave of pleasure quaking through me.

He moans my name into my ear, teeth roughly grazing my earlobe.

Here, tangled in Liam's sheets, I can't tell where I end and he begins... and I've never felt more complete.

## CHAPTER FIVE

# Liam

I wake early, as I'm used to.

Outside my window, the sky is still dark. The room is quiet... aside from the soft breathing of the beautiful young woman in my arms.

Ava still rests peacefully, her chest softly rising and falling, the blanket perfectly draping over her delicate figure. She looks so beautiful I can't resist the urge to lean down and hungrily press my mouth to hers.

Her eyelashes flutter, dark eyes cracking open as a sleepy smile spreads over her face.

"I thought it was a dream," she whispers. "A wonderful, sexy dream..."

I laugh and kiss her again. She sighs, arms looping around my neck to bring me closer. I wrap her up against me, hands splaying down her back so that I can gently cup the curve of her ass.

She fits perfectly against me, so much so that I can't convince myself to let go even though I know I have to leave to catch my flight.

I pull away from her lips only when I'm sure her lungs must be begging for air. "If it was a dream, it was the best one I've ever had." It's still extremely early, far too early for even a trace of sunlight to peek up above the horizon, and I don't want to disturb the twilight's stillness. "I have to leave for my flight, but you stay here and sleep. Just lock the door when you leave."

I wasn't worried about her getting into anything. There's something entirely trustable about Ava. When I look into those eyes of hers, I see nothing but genuine goodness. It's such a rare quality these days. Besides, I wasn't a materialistic man. I didn't have anything too valuable to try and make off with.

"Thanks," she murmurs. Her voice is still thick with sleep.

She sits up, grabbing a napkin off my dresser and scribbling something on it.

"This is my number," she says shyly. "Call me when you get back?"

I take it, gripping it in my hand tight. I cup her cheek with my other hand, pressing a kiss to her forehead.

"I'll call you way before that," I promise.

She blushes and giggles faintly. With that, I start to dress.

I'd long packed already, and it was simply a matter of pulling on some clothes and heading out the door.

Before leaving, I sink down to kiss her again. We hold one another tight. Her fingers stroke through my hair as I clutch her against me. One kiss isn't quite enough, so I kiss her again... and again.

After making sure that napkin was tucked into my pocket, I reluctantly head out the door. Before shutting it behind me, I turn back to gaze at her one last time. She's still sitting upright, the moon's silver glow dancing over her curves. Her eyes meet mine, silently begging for me to return to her.

With all my heart, I wish I could stay in that room with her. I wish I could turn off time and just escape into that bed.

Being intimate with Ava, being one with her, it felt so right. I'd never considered myself to have a certain type when it came to women, but Ava checked every single box I didn't even know I wanted. She might only be twenty-one, but she's ambitious and full of hope. To be so young and in the midst of opening her own business, that's inspiring.

The whole way to the airport, all I think about is her. I can't wait until we're back from pulverizing the Taranaki team so that we can be together again.

An hour later, I'm seated at the airplane terminal. Everyone is there, including Ryder, surprisingly enough, though he looks only semi-coherent. If there was anyone on the team who had too much fun, it would be that bloke. He's lucky his best friend, Kai, looks out for him.

"Flight 765 to New Plymouth is now boarding," the stewardess at the gate announces with a smile way too buoyant for this early hour.

As we head toward the gate, I brush a hand against my back pocket, expecting to feel the soft napkin against my fingers – instead, I feel nothing but the fabric of my pants.

Instantly, my stomach flips. I whirl around with a gasp, wildly looking up and down the airport terminal.

There isn't a sign of the napkin with Ava's number on it anywhere.

It's gone.

My heart thuds in my chest. I want to run back and do everything I can to find that tiny scrap of paper... but I have to get on the plane. My team needs me. I'd lost the National Cup once when I was a player, I wouldn't let the men on the team down as their coach.

Every minute is going to be excruciating... but I can only hope that Ava is still waiting for me when I return.

## CHAPTER SIX

# Ava

The bench is rough beneath me as I sink down upon it. My heart is just too heavy for me to stand anymore.

Biting my lip hard, I stare down at the Auckland newspaper gripped hard in my hands.

A weekly tradition, I'd picked up the paper for my old-fashioned grandmother... but what I hadn't expected was to see a picture of the Auckland rugby team right there on the front page.

Some up and coming journalist named Piper had written a story about the team alongside an interview she did with one of the players, and now I'm forcefully reminded that the team has returned from their victory in New Plymouth and Liam still hasn't called.

I don't know why I'm surprised.

I'm so young and he's so respected, established, and mature. What could he have really seen in me? I was surely just a torrid one-night affair that he'll laugh about with his buddies.

Still, I don't regret it. He made me feel things I never have before, things I'll never forget for the rest of my life.

When my phone vibrates, I answer it without glancing at the number.

"Ava speaking," I murmur, anticipating another cake order. Since quitting my job at the restaurant, the orders have come in slowly but surely, though a little more slowly and not quite as surely as I'd hoped.

Would I even make it as a baker? My dad had always encouraged me to take risks, but perhaps this was a risk that would never pay off.

"G'day, Ava!" someone says cheerfully. "You entered our contest for free tickets to the final National Cup game held here in Auckland over the weekend. You're our lucky grand prize winner! The tickets will be waiting for you at the ticket box the day of. Go Auckland!"

I collapse back against the bench, slapping my hand against my forehead. I'd completely forgotten I even entered that contest.

"Seriously?" I groan.

The radio hosts scoffs. "Well, you don't have to sound so depressed about it-"

I drop the phone, hanging up. My head lolls back against the bench.

My heart is suddenly torn in two.

My dad and I always said if Auckland played in the final round of the National Cup again, that we would go, that we *had* to go. I'd been able to ignore that dream because my finances have been so tight since quitting waitressing and starting up my baking business... but now I have free tickets and no excuse not to turn up at the game in my dad's old jersey.

I know I have to go and live out this dream for my father... but how am I going to work up the nerve to be near Liam again?

CHAPTER 7

# Liam

The players race across the field at such a breakneck speed that I can hardly keep up.

The National Cup has finally arrived, and I know every single man on my team is doing his best.

Jax is a blur, his face pinched with deep concentration. Ryder and Kai rush alongside him, trying to steal the ball from the other team. My head swivels back and forth from the field to the dwindling timer. There are minutes – seconds – left in the game. Every now and then Gray flies by, his lean figure lightning quick. Manu, slower but slower, is always there when needed.

This is it, what our entire season has hinged upon. The game is a clutch one, the scores so close that either team could take the lead.

One drop goal. That's all we need. It's all they need. But who will get there first?

Even though I know I should be solely focused on the game, thoughts of Ava continue to resurface in my mind.

I'd been trying to find her since returning from New Plymouth. My sister hadn't kept Ava's number from when she booked the cake, and when I went to the restaurant, they would only tell me that Ava wasn't working there anymore. I'd chased every lead I could and called dozens of local bakeries, but no one could point me toward the woman I yearned for so badly.

This should be the best day of my life, but there's a part of my heart that feels empty and bleak without her.

And what must she think about me? Did she think I'd forgotten about her?

I'd told her that I would call. I'd always been a man of my word.

Frustration pulses in me anew.

I'd met a woman who made my heart burst with joy. She made me feel like a new person, like I still had so much life to live... and I'd lost her because of my own carelessness. I should've been more careful with that bloody napkin.

How would I ever move on? Everywhere I go, I look for her. I listen for her familiar laugh. I hunt for those deep brown eyes.

I'd give anything to have her in my arms again.

Suddenly, the ball flies through the air toward the towering goal. Jax reels backward slightly, having just been the one to launch it.

I lurch forward, throat going tight. I hadn't been paying attention. This could be it, the make it or break it moment.

Would it go through the goal?

A strange hush falls over the stadium as everyone freezes, eyes locked on the ball. No one moves an inch. Even the wind seems to have stalled.

The ball rockets over the heads of the players on the field – finally flying through the goals.

The Auckland team explodes with joy as the final seconds of the timer dwindle and the ref whistles the game over. They jump around, grabbing each other and hollering with joy.

We'd done it!

We'd won the National Cup.

I can hardly believe it. All those hours spent training. My past injury. The days and weeks we'd devoted to rugby. It'd finally all paid off.

"Coach, Coach, Coach!" chants the team as they circle me. They continue to jump up and down as our fans hoot and holler with ecstatic joy.

I grin at them, trying to muster up the same enthusiasm they surely feel. I know I should be overwhelmed with joy. This should be my crowning moment, the one I'd been waiting for my whole professional life...

And yet, it's not the trophy I want to see. It's Ava's beautiful face.

Just as suddenly as they pounced on me, the team releases me.

"I think someone wants to talk to you, Coach," chuckles Kai as he nods his head behind me.

I turn slowly, jaw dropping when I see Ava behind me.

She wrings her hands, biting her lip. She's wearing a worn but cozy-looking jersey that's far too big for her... and she looks dazzling.

"Liam..." she says haltingly. "You didn't call, but... but I felt like I had to come watch the game."

I don't say anything. Words feel so useless in this moment. There are so many bloody emotions flying through me and pulsing in my heart, and I can't be sure how to put those feelings into words.

I need to hold her again. I need to make things right.

# Ava

I exhale sharply, eyes rounding as Liam slowly begins to stride toward me. He moves in slow motion, his powerful body looming ever closer.

All I'd wanted was to offer some congratulations to the Auckland coach, but now I'm rooted in place by Liam's gaze.

His eyes are narrowed, an intense combination of joy, relief, and shock swirling in those handsome orbs. I still don't know why he didn't call me like he said he would, but his expression is too sincere to be faked. I'd watched Liam while Jax made that final drop goal. I'd seen Liam smile when his team came to celebrate... but he hadn't looked this radiantly happy until he saw me.

As he moves closer, I'm drawn toward him like a moth to fire. It's impossible to resist the urge to rush forward. My legs move on their own, catapulting me over the grass.

I leap up into his arms and he spins me, clutching me against him as though it'd been years since we last embraced instead of just weeks. He sets me down, cupping my face as he presses his forward to mine.

The stadium is still going crazy because of the intense climax of the neck and neck game, but Liam hardly even seems to remember where we are at all.

"I lost the damn napkin, Ava," he whispers in a guttural, husky voice. His mouth is at my ear, his breath hot. "I tried to find you everywhere, but it was bloody impossible. I swear I wasn't going to give up. I was going to find you."

Tears of relief sting my eyes. "Now you don't have to find me... I'm here, Liam. I'm not going anywhere."

A grin brightens his face. He laughs, dragging me against him again.

In front of every single person in that stadium, he kisses me. The kiss is deep and rough and yet still perfectly tender. Again and again, his lips descend on mine. Butterflies swirl in my stomach, making me dizzy.

"I've missed you so much, Ava," he continues. He keeps touching me, pressing his fingers against my face and running his hand through my hair and embracing me tightly as though he isn't convinced I'm actually standing beside him. "I knew today was going to be special, but I had no idea just how special it would be. We right have won the National Cup... but all I care about is the fact that I've finally got you again."

My cheeks burn red as I bury my face against this strong shoulder, his arms still hooked tight around me, pressing me against his chest so that I can feel his heart beating with exuberant joy. I'm so happy that I can hardly stand it.

I'd found the man of my dreams and I'd witnessed firsthand Auckland win the National Cup just like my dad always wished. My heart is bursting with happiness.

Again, Liam pulls back slightly so he can gaze into my eyes.

"Today is the best day of my life, Ava," he says with a wide grin. "The bloody best day ever."

"It's the best day ever for me too!" I giggle, allowing him to spin me around again.

I bask in the jubilations of the stadium, in Liam's laughter, in the feeling of his arms around me.

This day is wonderful, delightful, and bright... but I know we're going to have a whole lot more of these joyous moments to share.

EPILOGUE

# Liam

The door chimes as Ava and I step over the threshold. She gives an immediate cry of delight, her hands clapping against her cheeks.

I wrap my arms around her waist, pulling her back against my chest as we both gaze around her new bakery. The finishing touches had just been put on it and we were getting to see it in all of its glory for the first time.

"It's more wonderful than I ever could've imagined!" she gushes, turning in my embrace to wrap her arms around my neck. "What do you think, Liam?"

"It's perfect," I answer with a grin. I kiss her on the lips before scooping her up into my arms.

I carry her into the kitchen, setting her deftly on the counter so she can take in the gleaming, state of the art appliances that she'd be using to lavish Auckland with delicious treats. She rests her head against my shoulder, fingers twining with mine.

Several months had passed since we won the National Cup. A new season would be upon us soon, as would a new team of bright-eyed young athletes eager to win the trophy for Auckland a second time.

Ava had been baking nonstop while taking online and phone orders to save up money for this storefront, and it'd finally paid off.

"I've already got my first in house order!" she adds, eyes gleaming. "I get to bake the cake for Ryder's big day. That's exciting, hm?"

I laugh and nod.

It's so wild to think about how far my players have come over this season, and the ways that each of their lives had changed. When Ryder had prophetically announced this would be the season that changed everything, he was damn right.

Ava pulls me closer, her cheeks glowing pink. I lean down, pressing a kiss to her soft lips.

The kiss lingers, deepening slowly. Even though months have passed, every time I kiss Ava, it's better than the last. She might be younger than I am, but age is just a number. Our happiness has been immeasurable. The National Cup win, while momentous, has been dwarfed by the joy I feel just having Ava in my life.

"I love you, Liam," she says softly. The tip of her nose brushes against mine as a shy smile crosses her face. "I thought the best day of my life was the day you won the National Cup and we reunited... but the days have just gotten better and better."

I stroke a hand through her hair, her dark curls bouncing against my palm.

"I love you too, Ava," I murmur, hungrily stealing another sweet kiss. "My whole career, I thought I was just chasing success and a trophy... but in reality, I was looking for you. Every choice I made led me to your side."

She giggles, sliding closer to the edge of the counter to hook her legs around my waist and draw me closer. I lean down, pressing my lips against hers as the velvet tip of her tongue sweeps against my lower lip.

Just as she gives a seductive sigh, the tinkling bell at her bakery's door begins to jangle back and forth.

"Coach!" someone calls. "Coach! Ava! We're here to celebrate the bakery's opening!"

I roll my eyes. "Speaking of Ryder," I mutter with a chuckle.

A chorus of voices joins Ryder's loud one as the other members of my rugby team spill into the main entrance of the bakery.

Ava and I laugh as I help her off the counter and toward the front door. There, Jax, Kai, Manu, Gray, and Ryder are waiting, as is the rest of the team.

They crowd around us, eagerly chatting and making comments about the pretty bakery, but Ava and I are still lost in one another's eyes.

This, I reckon, is what true bliss feels like.

I'm surrounded by friends, and at the side of a woman I love with my whole heart. It doesn't get any better than this.

Of all the trophies I've won and all the victories I've reveled in, the greatest prize I've ever won is Ava and the future she and I now get to share.

I can't wait to see what tomorrow will bring Ava and me – and the whole Auckland team. If there's one thing I'm bloody sure of, it's that all of our lives will be brimming with love and happiness from here on out.

The End

# ABOUT THE AUTHOR

Eva writes short, sweet but steamy romance stories! A true romantic at heart, Eva lives in West Australia but is still a down-to-earth Kiwi. She loves strong, sensitive men in her real life and in her stories! Eva has a whole load of "Down Under" steamy romance stories lined up for you - from rugged rugby players to firefighting Australian Alphas :)